Meeting An Alpha

Brianne May

Contents

Chapter 1 - Mate?

 ***

Walking around in this tan painted building didn't help my mission to figure this fudging place out. It was bigger than I expected or atleast bigger than the website said. Mentally I was sculpting a map but with this place I might as well do a better job in the Amazon rainforest. Even though I look very young for my age, most people guess me about 17 or 18, I am in fact a teacher, not a student. And this is the very first high school I would be teaching at, since I got out of collage. Nervous is not even the word I can use to describe my feelings. Instead of butterflies playing in my tummy, it was goblins throwing a party and dancing on my insides.

When I finally found my homeroom the kids were chatting about not noticing me enter, I took a couple of minutes to look around. The previous teacher didn't care to look after it because some of the paint was peeling off and the colors was bland. I made a mental note to brighten up the place.

"Kids" My voice was a little louder than I wanted it to be. They starred at me confused but obeyed my authority and took their seats. I mentally smiled at this reaction, this was going good so far.

"I will be your new homeroom and English teacher" I silently praise myself for my confidence taking in a deep breath before I begin marking down the names of kids who are attended.

"John Williams" I call out, nobody answers.

"John?" I repeat. Still no answer. I let out a big sigh and was about to mark him as absent when the door swung open. A young boy stepped in. Quite handsome for his age, with dark hair and chocolate brown eyes. I knew this kid was going to be a trouble maker.

"Who are you?" My voice sounded strict. He returned with a smirk.

"Williams, John Williams." He replied trying his best at a James Bond accent.

"Well mister 007, consider this your first and last warning, I won't be so nice next time, please take your seat." Again praising myself for my confidence.

"With pleasure, mam." He was still smirking, taking his seat next to a red head girl, wearing an outfit that barely covers her privates.

*****Luckily the morning went by fast and it was time for lunch. I walked into the teacher lounge and was greeted by a lot of elder teachers. Finally I spotted a young girl near my age. In school I didn't have much confidence, so I would never just walk to someone and 'just make friends,' but as time passed I learned to be more confident. Or so I thought.

"Hi" I smiled at the perky dark haired girl. She was quite beautiful. She had almost golden eyes. It was a complete contrast with my piercing blue eyes. My hair was also dark but had a purple glimmer in them. I liked to be different so I coloured my coffee brown hair. She was also very skinny, were I was curvy, which was both a blessing and a curse.

"Hi!" She smiled back happily. That's a good start.

"I am Lea, new here."

"Thought so" she giggled. "Anne"

"Nice to meet you." I smiled. "I finally know one person besides the students.

" Yeah they can be a handful" she laughed.

"Especially this one, I think his name was...uh....John?"

She let out a deep laugh.

"What?" I suddenly felt embarrassed.

"That's my younger brother. If you think he is bad, you should meet my older one. " There was still a laugh in her words.

"Oh. Sorry" I said still feeling embarrassed.

"Forget about it, sometimes I think I am the only normal one around here." We both laughed.

"So is it only you three?"

"No, I have a older sister as well. But she left when I was young. She and my dad didn't get along very well. She fell in love and he didn't like it."

"That's really sad" I felt sorry for her.

"Yeah, but when my brother took over the family business things changed. He was wiser with his decisions. But more cold. My sister didn't want to return. The man she fell for was direct competition. I think a part of her felt he was like my dad, even though he isn't, he wouldn't let his company be threatened."

"Sounds serious. This family business."

"Yeah after my dad dies my brother took over. At age 19, he was the youngest...uh owner of the company."

"Sounds like a incredible man"

"He is. Too bad he is a bit of a douche" she laughed.

***** The rest of the day went by fast. I gathered my stuff and went by Anne's class to say goodbye. When I arrived I heard loud voices outside the door.

"I will not return to the house!" This was Anne, she sounded mad.

"I am not telling you, I am ordering you to." A deep calm male's voice sounded.

"Well I don't care!"

"Can't you for once in your life just listen to me. It is safer at the house."

"I can't leave my mate now, you know that. And since you refuse to have him in your house, I will not be returning, thank you."

Mate?

Confused I decided to leave. There was something pulling me towards the door but I ignored it. It would be rude to interrupt Anne and whoever she was talking to.

A few steps away the door swung open and as compelled as I was to turn around and look who it was she was talking to, I just kept on walking.

***** Later that night, while resting on my bed with my laptop, I thought of Anne. Mate? Like friends? Must be. But why would she not leave him? No Lea this has nothing to do with you just finish your preparations. I started working further on my preparations for tomorrow. Mate? I sighed deeply knowing I am not going to win this war. I will just ask Anne tomorrow. But then she will think I am some kind of stalker? No just asked her.

******

Chapter 2 - Meeting a Greek god!

I grown as my alarm clock goes off. It's my second day and I am already tired. I sat up from my bed, but had this cold feeling I am being watched. I shake it off, grabbed my towel and walked into my tiny bathroom. Yeah, having a tiny flat comes with tiny bathrooms. I opened the warm water and let it graze my skin. Feeling utterly refreshed I got out of my shower and walked towards my cupboard. No, I didn't have a walk in closet.

I took out a fresh pair of black lace lingerie and got dressed in a washed blue skinny jean with a dress shirt. Put on a little mascara and eye liner and was ready to face the world.

*****I arrived early at school with not a lot of teachers that are in yet. I decided to see if Anne was around. With just the right amount of luck she was sitting at her desk.

"Hey" I greeted

"Hi, Lea!" She smiled up at me, she seemed in a better mood.

"You sound happy?"

"Yeah my..uh..husband....brought me breakfast in bed this morning." She smiled.

"Oh...I didn't know you were married?"

"Yeah..I...Yeah" she looked down and continued scribbling on a piece of paper.

"So I better get going then?"

"Oh sorry Lea, I was just in thought"

"Does it have something to do with the man you were talking to yesterday?"

"Excuse me?!"

"Oh sorry! I just heard you arguing with someone and left."

"How much did you hear?" She was suddenly defensive.

"Just something about a mate...and someone wanting you to move in...and that's about it."

"Sorry" she sighed. "That was my brother. He has this way of making me so mad!"

"That's why I am glad I am the only child." I tried to lighten the mood.

"Yeah" she looked down.

"Anne can I ask you something?"

"Shoot!"

"What did you mean by mate?"

"Uh...it's kinda a....a nickname for my husband" she laughed nervously.

"Mate? As in a animals mate?"

"Yeah he loves wolves!"

"Oh makes sense. But I better get going. See you lunch time."

"See ya"

******

"John Williams, you are late again." I scowled.

"Sorry" he mumbled.

"That's it! I warned you. I want a 2000 word essay on being on time on my desk tomorrow morning!"

"You can't do that!"

"I sure as hell can!" This kid was getting on my nerves.

"Just because you don't...." He was interrupted by a knock on the door.

"Enter" I said rubbing my temples.

I felt the person enter the room. Without looking up I felt a sensation in my stomach, almost like butterflies. My body felt warm all over. I looked up to be greeted by golden orbs. Almost like Anne's just more perfect. Yep those are butterflies. A Greek god was standing in front of me. He had a very muscular chin, with dark hair and tanned skin. His body was fit and lean through what I can see in his tight shirt. He was dressed very formal. And it looked HOT!

"C..Can I help you?" I shuttered.

He had a attractive smirk on his face. Clearly amused by my reaction.

"I am here to pick up my brother?"

"Sorry?" I was completely confused. He moved closer and nodded his head in the direction of John.

"Oh? May I ask why?" I didn't want to argue with this amazing creature but nobody takes my students away without a reason.

"A doctors appointment." He smirked.

"Uh..okay sure." I frowned. It didn't make sense sending a boy to school only to pick him up so early for a doctors appointment.

"Nathan." He said stretching out his hand towards me.

"Lea" I smiled gladly shaking it. As soon as I touched it sparks of electricity flooded by body. My knees was about to go weak.

"Guess I will see you around, sweetheart." He winked and walked out the door. John following him and almost laughing at my red face.

***** "How old is your brother?" I said sitting next to Anne.

"Uhh 16?" She said frowning.

"No the other one!"

"Oh Nathan, about 26 why?"

"Just asking" I said smirking thinking about it.

"Shut up! You like him!" She squealed.

"Well he looks like a Greek god!!" I exclaimed throwing my hands up in the air. That earned a lot of shhh coming from the elder teachers.

"Lea" she sighed. "You should probably stay away from him. He is kind of bad news."

"No it's nothing like that. It's just when we touched. Ugh it was electricity." I sat back taking in the feeling.

"Fuck" Anne's face was now turning very pale.

"Anne?" I was concerned "you okay?"

"Yeah..I just have to..make a call." She got up and walked out taking out her phone.

Okay?

*****The rest of the day seemed to go by very long. I finally reached my car. I was still a bit worried about Anne. She looked like she was going to faint.

"Hey" A voice said behind me. It sounded kind of familiar. I turned to a blue eyes man with blond hair. He was one of the teachers. I have seen him around.

"Hey" I smiled at him. He was kind of attractive.

"Alex" He stretched out his hand. I grabbed it and shook it.

"Lea"

"I have been meaning to talk to you, but these first few days of school are hectic." He grabbed the back of his neck.

"Yeah" I let out a nervous laugh. Pull yourself together!

"So..uh if you need someone to show you around..I would gladly play tour guide."

"Thanks, I would definitely need that" Good Lea.

"Good" he had a smile on his face. "So enjoy your day."

"You too"

I still couldn't shake that feeling of being watched.

Just as I was about to start my car, my phone buzzed.

Anne: Dinner, Friday, 7pm, my place. You better be there!

Me: Sure :).

And I drove home without waiting for a response.

Chapter 3 -You are mine

The rest of the week went by fast and Friday finally came. I was very excited to have dinner at Anne's place. The more I got to know her, the more I got interested in her life. She had it rough, she explained. They all did. Her eldest brother the most because he had to take over the family business. Her eldest sister tried to make contact with them after her fathers death but her lover wouldn't have it. The feud was to strong.

After I got out the shower I decided to wear a black wrap dress with a bit of heels. I liked dressing up, even if its just for dinner. I grabbed the cheap bottle of wine I got earlier and headed to the address Anne gave me.

When I arrived I was greeted by a male with brown buzzed cut hair and greenish eyes.

"Jason Anderson" he nodded.

"Lea Jackson." I nodded back.

"Lea, you found it!" Anne came to hug me. "I was worried, it is so far out town."

"Thank you GPS." I laughed.

"Sit down, your timing is perfect dinner is ready!"

I took my seat and Anne immediately started a conversations about teens and their obsessions.

"I mean remember the whole twilight thing going around!" She threw her hands up.

"I never really watched or read twilight." I felt slightly embarrassed.

"Really? First woman ever." Jason laughed.

"Yeah, I never really liked the idea of vampires and werewolves."

"Why not?" Anne frowned.

"Because it's kind of silly. I mean a person turning into a wolf or a bat."

"Well vampires don't really..." Jason was stopped by a cold stare from Anne.

"Well I thinks it's romantic." Anne said.

"How can dating a dog be romantic." That sounded a lot more harsh then I wanted it to. Jason burst out laughing.

"She's got a point babe." He winked at her. Anne growled at him.

"Well a werewolf gets a mate picked for them by the moon goddess. And with that that mate stays forever. And no one can feel exactly like the bond that a wolf has with his mate. Or so I read."

"Sounds cheesy!" I rolled my eyes. "I mean no one can forever love someone it's just impossible."

Anne muttered something under her breath but I couldn't quite make it out.

"So when are you two having kids?" I tried to change the subject. The room fell silent. Jason's face saddened while Anne looked down.

"I..I can't have kids." Anne said sadly. My heart broke.

"I am so sorry Anne."

"We learned to accept it." Jason mentioned. And the room went silent again. What a idiot! I was mentally slapping myself in the face.

That feeling in my stomach rose again. There was a knock on the door. Anne went to open it.

"We have a problem!" Nathan burst in. His face immediately shot to where I was sitting and a smile was forming on his marvellous lips.

"Hi" I almost whispered.

"Hi beautiful." He winked and after a few seconds of staring turned his attention back to Anne. "Can we talk privately?"

"Yeah in the study."

"I'll be joining" Jason got up.

"No! You got a guest, this is family matters" Nathan growled.

After they left I saw my chance.

"Whats the deal with you and Nathan?" I asked bluntly.

Jason sighed.

"When we were in high school we both liked a girl, Mia, I got her and that made Nathan hate me. What made it worse was the fact that I broke her heart when I met Anne. Anne was my one true soulmate. I guess he never really got over it."

I don't know why but I felt extremely jealous and mad right now. Just then Anne and Nathan returned. Anne not looking very impressed.

"So are you going to invite me to join or what?" Nathan asked smugly making eye contact with me. Before anybody got a chance to answer he sat down next to me. A lot closer than I would have liked. Shivers went down my spine as our thighs touched. He bluntly put his arm at the back of my chair and started talking. I couldn't figure out about what because I was too busy focusing on our thighs.

"Wouldn't you say Lea?" Anne asked. My head shot back upwards.

"W..what?" This earned a smirk from Nathan.

"Don't be so shy beautiful." He whispered in my ear. I could feel his breath on my neck. Oh what he could do to me with those lips.

"Lea!" Anne tried again.

"Sorry?" I couldn't stop my face from turning red.

"I said it was time to pour us some of that wine you brought."

"Oh yeah."

Anne had almost a knowing smile on her face, while Nathan seemed to be completely amused by these events. Jason on the other hand was staring like a lovesick puppy at Anne.

After dinner and wine I wanted to go home. Being around Nathan made me nervous. I said my goodbyes and to my complete irritation Nathan insisted on walking me to my car.

"You look beautiful, beautiful." He smiled checking me out.

"Thanks" I mumbled.

"Don't ever wear that dress again." He said firm.

What?

"What!?"

"I don't want other guys checking you out." His voice made it sound obvious.

"And why should I care what you want." I was pissed off now.

He took a few steps closer. I tried to move back but the car was blocking my way. He lend in until I could feel his warm breath tickling my neck. My legs wanted to give out under me. I didn't even notice was holding my breath.

"Because you're mine." He softly but seductively whispered in my ear.

Chapter 4 - Seer

After I got home, I lied on my bed trying to figure out the events that had just occurred. His words were rolling inside my head. Mine. He was so sure of himself. As if he just bought me. How can one man with such a beautiful face,have such an ego! My phone buzzed.

Unknown: Be ready tomorrow at 6pm. N

N? As in Nathan? How did he get my phone number!? It buzzed again

Alex: Hey was wondering if we could meet up for coffee tomorrow?

Me:Sure! :)

****The sun is so sharp. I only got in an hour of sleep. I kept dreaming of a wolf. The odd thing about him was that he was completely red. Like a blood red color. He wasn't chasing me, he was rather trying to play with me. But suddenly he got mad, he was growling but not at me at something behind me. When I turned around I was faced with a big black wolf. He looked harmful. He was about to launch himself towards me, when I woke up. This kept on going on the entire night. I open the door of the café when I saw those blue eyes stare at me. There was a huge smile on his face.

"Hey" I smiled at him.

"Hey. I ordered already if that's okay"

"No problem Alex, I am sorry for the way I look, I just didn't get much sleep last night."

"What? You look perfect."

"Thanks." My cheeks turned red.

"How was your night last night? Anne told me you were going to dinner."

"Uh odd." I chuckled.

"Really why?"

"Anne brother Nathan showed up." I said rolling my eyes.

"Oh him" Alex looked tense.

"You okay?"

"Yeah, It's just I don't like him very much."

"How come?"

"He just walks around as if he owns the town." Now Alex was rolling his eyes

"Yeah I noticed his ego."

"But hey lets not talk about him" Alex reached out and touched my hand. Something inside me had a urge to pull away. But instead I just smiled and left it there.

******It was around 5pm and I was busy complicating whether I should get ready for Nathan or stream on Netflix. Hmmm. He can't hurt me can he? Maybe not. But maybe yes? Uggg just go with the guy! No! He could be a serial killer! Your being pathetic. Sometimes I hate my inner voice. Fine!

I got up and got dressed, nothing fancy tho, I didn't want to impress him. Or did I?

I heard a car pull up outside. Suddenly nerves hit me. I checked my watch. Exactly 6pm. I went to the door but already found him inside. He turned to look at me and my heart melted.

"Hi beautiful." He smirked.

"Hey." I was slightly irritated by now.

"Ready?" He opened his arm for me to lock onto it, instead I ignored him and kept on walking. I got into the passenger seat of his 718 Boxster Porsche. He got in next to me with a sigh and started the car. We arrived at a very fancy restaurant, one where I know I would never be able to afford.

When we entered, everybody was nodding their heads down, clearly a sign of respect. The whole place was cleared out. There was only one table in the middle where the candle was lit. Nathan lead me towards the table and we both took our seats.

"I am not a bad guy you know"

" that's not what I heard." I saw a glint of sadness in his face but he quickly shook that away.

"I'll prove it to you then." He suggested.

"Challenge accepted." I had a smug smile on my face.

"You look tired beautiful." He was staring straight into my eyes.

"I am." I sighed.

"Didn't you sleep." There was concern in his voice

"No."

"Why?"

I kept thinking whether I should tell him about the dream or not. I gave in and told him. He had a deep frown on his face.

"Is it the first time, you are dreaming such dreams?"

"No." I confessed. "As a kid I had a lot of dreams like that, just not of the red wolf." He was still frowning, deep in thought.

"Are you okay?"

"Hmm, it's just seems like something."

"Like what?"

"You wouldn't believe me, even if I told you, beautiful."

"Try me." I was now determined.

"Well between my people someone like you is called a seer. It is a very rare gift."

" Your people?" Now I am confused.

He let out a deep sigh."I am a werewolf, and I believe you are too. I don't know why your wolf had been hiding from you, but it's true. That voice inside your head? That's her.

But you aren't just any werewolf, you are a seer. The rarest of the wolf ranks. When you enter a pack you would have a mental connection with them. You can mind speak and read their minds regardless of the distance. You receive visions that's helps the shamans, a very magical wolf, to make accurate predictions. Not all packs are blessed with a seer. Probably why you have been living as a rough, also known as a lone wolf, for so long."

I couldn't believe what I am hearing. I started laughing but soon stopped when I saw his face. He was serious!

"Then what are you in this so called pack?"

"The alpha. Meaning the leader. And soon you will join my pack."

"Well since you said that not all packs have seer, I can join any pack I wish. Why would I join yours?"

"Because not only are you a seer, you are also my mate and future Luna of my pack."

chapter 5 - Be safe Lea

I could have sworn my face was turning white. Luna? Pack? No!

"This is not true."

"Lea" Nathan reached out to grab my hand. A spark of electricity filled my body. I removed my hand from his immediately.

"Your lying"

"Don't you feel that?" He looked straight into my eyes. "Don't you feel us?"

I couldn't respond.

"Listen we don't....."

"I want to meet you pack" yes that came out firm.

"What?" His brows furrowed.

"I. Want. To. Meet. Your. Pack. If what your saying is true. I got to see your pack."

"You can't" I could hear anger in his voice.

"And why not?" My voice started to get louder.

"Because your a rough! If they see you now they would kill you without thinking. I must mate and mark you first."

Mark? Mate!

"What?"

He sighed. "When a wolf meets his mate, he marks her. To show all the unmated males she is his. The mark takes place during...well...mating, it is very intimate. If wolf marks someone without mating it would be very painful. As Alpha when I mark...."

"If!"

"Sorry?"

"If you mark me."

"When I mark you, you will become Luna of my pack and that creates a bond, with both me and you, and you and my pack. You become like a mother to them."

"And if I won't let you mark me?"

"You can't. The mates pull is strong, especially when it comes from a Alpha. If you keep on fighting it, it will hurt me and you. We will grow weaker. Until we both get so depressed we wouldn't want to live without our mate. As a result we can become more heartless"

"And if I love someone else?" I could see him tense at my words.

"You can't. He would never make you happy. He can never make you feel like I can."

"Can I...can I see your wolf?"

"Not right now, beautiful. I wouldn't be able to control him. He wants you. He won't stop until he get you."

"Oh"

"As I was saying, we don't have a lot of time. Your dreams are a warning. And I think I know of what."

"Of what?"

"There was an Alpha of another pack not far away from here. Lucius was his name. He was merciless. He even killed members of his own pack, just for the fun of it. Under an Alpha you get a Beta, second in command. Under a Beta is a Delta, training to be Beta. In that pack, they had a very brave Delta called Sam.

Now Sam grew tired of Lucius and decided to create a rebellion in the pack. They over thrown Lucius. But he was strong. He killed half of the pack including Sam. The Beta had thrown him and those who were loyal to him out of the territory.

Rumor has it he is creating his own pack of rogues. When he hears of a seer nearby he would want her for his pack. He would want you. Probably even try to mark you.

I think your dream has something to do with that. A red wolf resembles an Alpha, the strength of the Alpha is also shown by the shade of the red."

The wolf was a very deep shade of red. Almost mahogany.

" I am guessing, black means rough?"

"No. A rough is brown. Like a normal wolf. Black resembles an wolf who had killed his mate."

"Killed his mate?"

"Some wolves do it." Nathan sighed. I could see pain in his face. " Even though a mate can make a wolf grow stronger, they are also a weakness."

Weakness? I felt something inside me growl.

"Yes." Nathan looked down. "A wolf cannot battle knowing his mate is in danger. That's why some kill their mates. It makes them bitter and hollow. But it also makes them strong. They have no worries. No regrets."

"That's horrible!"

"That's why I want to mark you as fast as I possibly can. I am not rushing you. I am just saying we don't have a lot of time Lea."

"I...I want to think about it."

He nodded.

"We have to spend a lot of time together as well. The more time you spend with me, the stronger our bond grows. If it grows stronger you would not have such a strong rough smell. Then you can move into the pack house and we can take care of you. The pack doesn't have to know about you until I marked you. You would simply look like a omega, the lowest of the pack"

"Move into the pack house? No! No! And hell no!"

"Lea, it's for your own safety."

"We don't even know if what you are saying would happen."

"It will. I can set you up with the shaman tomorrow and she can confirm it to you."

I sighed. "Fine. I will think about it."

"Thank you" he was smiling at me.

"I want to go home now."

"Whatever your heart desires beautiful."

*****The ride back to my house was silent. When we got out, Nathan walked me to my door.

"Goodnight" I said before opening my door.

He stepped closer to me. I could feel the heat radiating off him. My body wanted to be in his arms. I wanted him to hold be close. He put his hands on my sides and looked down at me. Was he going to kiss me? He starred me into my eyes. I could feel his breath on me. He lifted his chin and placed a tiny kiss on my forehead.

"Be safe Lea." With that he turned and walked to his car. My body was about to melt.

chapter 6 - Learn our kind

I was woken by a knock on the door. It sounded urgent. Putting on a robe I walked towards the door and opened it.

"We have to get you out of here." Nathan rushed in.

"What why?"

"Lucius is in town."

"And?"

"There is rumors going around he paired up with the witches. They would sense you. He would want you."

"Look I am a big..."

"I will not argue with Lea. Go get your stuff." I could see the anger boiling inside of him.

"Okay! Where are we going?"

"The pack house."

"I thought you said they would kill me."

"I would rip all their heads off, if it meant I can protect you." He grabbed my arm softly.

"Okay." I breathed out.

*****When we got to the pack house there was a lot of stares and growls heading my way. Some moved closer but no one dares to harm the Alpha's guest. At least not yet.

Nathan lead me into a big bedroom. He told me to freshen up and come to dinner. When he left I studied the room. It was filled with paintings. They looked beautiful but I didn't recognized the painter. Very classy room. I could get use to this. After freshening up I headed down stairs. When I arrived at the table I earned a lot of growls.

"Family, she is my guest, therefore you will respect her. If not I will rip your head of your body." Nathan spoke up and everybody quieted down.

I took a seat next to him. Somehow I felt safe next to him. The whole dining table was filled with food. I was starving.

The rest of the day went by fast. I met a couple of the pack members. I met Nathans Beta, Delta and a few Omega's working in the house. Nathan took me to meet the Shaman but she wasn't there. Probably out to get some herbs. I also meat someone they called Pi, apparently this is the packs therapist. They seemed to be less tense around me. Somehow I was thankful for that. I spoke to the Pi and he advised me on how to better fit into the pack. I wasn't sure on staying, but I might as well make myself comfortable here for the time being.

When nightfall came I headed to my room, only to find Nathan in it. He was only wearing a pair of boxers.

"What are you doing here?"

"This is my room." He shrugged.

"Then why am I here?"

"I sure as hell ain't leaving you out of my sight."

"And I sure as hell ain't sleeping next to you."

"Chill princesses, I will be taking the couch." He walked over to the couch. I hadn't notice the blanket and pillow on it. "For now" he winked as he lied on his back on the couch.

"Tomorrow we will start your training."

"Training as in fighting?"

"Training as in killing."

" I would love to find out how to kill you!" I chuckled. I could see a smile forming on his lips.

"You will not only find out how to kill a werewolf beautiful. You will also know how to kill a witch, vampire, and more. Even a Lycan."

"What's a Lycan?"

"It's like a werewolf. Just a lot stronger. I will explain tomorrow beautiful.
"

I rested my head against the pillow.

"Goodnight Nathan."

"Goodnight Lea."

****"Catch sweetheart!" This was Lou, he was one of the elders who agreed to train me. He was throwing a small gun at me.

"What am I to do with this."

"There are a lot of ways to kill a werewolf. A silver bullet to the heart is the easiest."

"What's the hardest way?"

"Depends if the wolf was born or cursed. If born the bullet. When in wolf form you can chop of a limb to revert the back to human and kill him like a normal human. Wolfsbane can also weaken a werewolf.

If cursed you can kneel in one spot for a hundred years than you will be transformed back into a human. You can also be called three times on you Baptist name while being struck three times on the forehead with a knife.

Some say a sword that is blessed on the altar of a chapel dedicated to Saint Hubert can kill a werewolf as well, but I think that's a rumor the humans created."

"You can be cursed into a werewolf?"

"Yes if you anger some of the elder witches they will curse you, or drinking the water of the tracks where a werewolf stepped. There is also a stream that flows. It has this whole chanting thing involved and drinking from the stream. There is a flower you can eat to become a wolf and my personal favorite a werewolf bite."

"I didn't know that."

"There's a lot you must learn from your kind little bird. But now you must learn to shoot. "

After a couple of rounds practicing and Lou teaching me hand to hand combat, Nathan walked in.

"Are you guys done yet?"

"I think that's enough for today." Lou said picking up a bottle of water.

"Come on beautiful, I have someone I want you to meet." Nathan grabbed my hand and let my out.

We entered his study where a elderly woman was standing. I am guessing it was Nathans mom by the golden eyes she had.

"Lea, this is my mom and the old Luna of this pack. I want you to learn from her because you never had a pack and don't know the duties of a Luna."

"Hi Mrs Williams." I extended my hand.

"A Luna never greets first. It respectful for a pack member to greet first." She said bluntly.

"Oh sorry." I looked down.

"Never look down. You second to the Alpha, you don't bow your head to anybody."

I looked up at her, furrowing my brows.

"I will leave you two to it then." Nathan started to retreat. "I'll see you tonight beautiful."

*****"She hates me!" I said throwing myself on the bed.

"She doesn't hate you. She was a woman of authority, she doesn't take it kindly teaching a vagabond."

"What did you call me?"

"Vagabond. In other words a lone wolf."

"Ohhh"

"Yes beautiful." Nathan was now starting to take off his shirt. I was mesmerized by his abs.

"I will never fit in." I pulled the pillow over my face.

"Of course you will. I will arrange that books of our kind be sent up here, so that you can study and learn to be one of us."

"Thank you" I smiled up at him.

Chapter 7 - Please be mine

The forest was thick and foggy. If It wasn't the burning inside my lungs from running I would have frozen to death. Then all of a sudden a big black wolf launched himself on top of me. His big canine teeth was now showing. He was staring at the space between my neck and shoulder. He came closer as if trying to bit. But suddenly fear filled his eyes. A golden wolf appeared by my side....

"Lea." I heard Nathan voice. My eyes shot open when I felt two strong hands grip my waist. Nathan was looking at me concerned.

"W..whats going on?"

"You were basically screaming."

"Oh" I didn't notice the tears streaming down my face.

"Lea" Nathan pulled me into a hug. I shifted my face deeper into his chest. His arms felt so right around me. I looked up into his eyes. He wasn't starring at my eyes, he was starring at my lips. My eyes shifted toward his. The distance between us suddenly became a lot closer. He leaned in, but instead of a deep, lustful kiss, it was a small gentle one he placed on my lips. I wanted more but he didn't comply.

"Once we start, I don't know if I would be able to end." He smiled at me gently cupping my chin so that I was looking him directly in eyes.

"Okay" I said trying to get up but his grip on waist only tightened.

"That doesn't mean we can't embrace each other for a couple of moments." I smiled and put my head back on his chest. He hugged me tight.

*****After Nathan insisted on taking me to school and placing a small kiss on my forehead. I walked in knowing I was completely unprepared. The events of the weekend had taken up all my attention.

"Lea hi!" Alex started walking towards me. He pulled me into a tight hug.

"Hi Alex."

"Listen I wanted to ask you for some time now. My friend has this band. And He keeps bugging me to go, so I wondered maybe you can help me out by joining?"

"Uhm Alex I got a lot on my plate by now. Maybe if it's all sorted out then yes."

"You can talk to me you know?"

"I know." I hugged him once again.

*****After I walked out the school waiting for Nathan to pick me up, I saw a man staring at me. He looked somewhat older than me, starting to turn grey. He had green orbs and the hair color that wasn't turning grey was black. He looked intimidating. He looked scary. We were just staring at each other.

"Hi beautiful." A voice said behind me. I turned and smiled at Nathan, while he pecked my lips. When I turned back at the guy, he was gone.

"What's wrong?"

"I thought I saw someone. He looked familiar." I didn't turn back to Nathan.

"It was probably nobody. Now come on I got something to show you." Nathan grabbed my arm.

We drove a while out of the city. Until we reached a clear open field on a mountain top. The sun was about to set. Nathan took out a blanket from the car and some snacks and wine.

"This place is very special to me." He said.

"How come?"

"My father used to bring me up here as a kid. Everybody knew him as the scary Alpha. So did I. But when we were here, he was just normal. We would chat about everything, until the sound went down and then we would cuddle up in a blanket and watched the stars." He was smiling at that memory.

"Thank you for sharing that, Sharing this.." I was holding my arms out at the space. "With me"

"No problem." He was looking me in the eyes. "But that's not why I brought you here."

I waited patiently for him to continue.

"I want you to be my mate. By your own free will." He pulled out a box, when he opened it there was a necklace inside. The necklace was made out of silver. It had a large rose stone and two smaller stones on it. The one small stone was a golden color and the other a greenish color.

"This belonged to my grandmother. She believed it will bring protection. She said a witches magic is held up in there. But I don't really believe. What I do believe that if you chose to be my mate, I want you to have it."

I didn't know what to say. He wanted me to choose to spend my entire life with him. And I want to. This perfection of a man want me, a plain old girl to be his. His! I was fixated on the necklace. It was beautiful. I want it. Maybe I can spend my entire life with this man. Maybe love at first sight does exist. Maybe one must learn to love. Whatever it was inside of me it was screaming for control and before I could stop my self I said it...

"I will be your mate!" We both starred at each other shocked. Until Nathan pulled me in for a kiss. This time more intense than the last. He licked my bottom lip for entrance which I gladly gave. Both our mouths flowed with each other. Entwined. His hand snaked around my waist pulling me closer to him. Until I was on top of him. He deepened the kiss. Holding me steady with one hand and playing with my hair with the other. It felt like the world can explode and I wouldn't notice. He pulled away. Still holding onto me.

"Thank you." He whispered, placing a kiss on my forehead.

Chapter 8 - The latin greeting

When we got home I could barely keep my eyes open. Nathan carried me bridal style up the stairs and into his room. He lied me on the bed and kissed me softly.

"Sleep now princess." He whispered.

"Boss we got a problem." Someone burst in. I couldn't open my eyes to look at who. I heard Nathan growl.

"What?" He sounded angry.

"Can we talk in private." I felt Nathan get up from the bed and walk away. The door closed softly.

After what felt like forever I heard the door open again. I felt a presence next to me on the bed and warm strong arms wrap around my waist. His breath was on my neck and his grip was strong.

"I love you." He said softly into my ear.

****The next morning felt like the best morning ever. I woke up with arms holding onto me. It was just any arms, it was the arms of my mate.

"Morning beautiful." His husky morning voice sounded. He looked so sleepy yet so sexy.

"Morning." I said lying my head on his chest, looking up at him.

"You look amazing."

"Amazing? I just woke up."

"Still naturally beautiful."

I leaned forward and started kissing him. He held me tight. He pulled away.

"I want to ask you something before you we start the day."

"Yeah?"

"I want to mark you."

"What?"

"Something's not right. I want you to be safe. And with my mark you will be a member of the pack. You can mind speak and warn of danger. I will also be able to sense your emotions and know when you are frightened. It is all your choice. I don't want to pressure you."

"Two major choices in two days." I laughed. "Of course you can mark me Nathan. I...I love you."

Nathan looked shocked for a moment. And then a smile spread across his face. "I love you too."

He rolled over to lay on top of me and started kissing me.

****When I arrived at school the only thing I could think about was the morning I had. I moved my hand to the place where Nathan marked me, I could still feel his teeth sink into me. I thought it would hurt, but it felt like pure ecstasy.

"Lea wait!" Alex came running towards me.

"Oh Alex hi." I stood still.

"On what world are you I kept calling you but no answer."

"Oh sorry." I blushed. I couldn't get Nathan off my mind.

"So do you think we can go to that band tonight?"

"I can't. I am kind of busy." His face changed it looked sad.

"Oh sorry for bothering you Lea." He started to walk away.

"No Alex." I called. He turned. "Please life just a bit complicated, next time okay?" I reassured him.

"Okay." He said upset and walked away.

****The parking lot was still. Nathan took his time picking me up. In the background I heard mumbling but no one was around.

"Hello." I called. No answer.

The mumbling got louder. It sounded Latin.

"This is not funny!" I yelled.

Louder and louder it got. It got so loud my ears almost hurt.

"Lupus enim nostrum." It repeated.

I turned around and still no one was to be seen. When I turned back I saw my source. A black hooded figure stood in front of me. I turned to run but another stood behind me. I was surrounded. They were everywhere.

"Well well well the little pup finally made her appearance. " A male voice said. He pushed himself forward between the crowd of hooded figures. I looked up at him. It was the same man I saw the other day.

"W...who are you?"

"I think you know the answer. " he crossed his arms. "But if you must know. They call me Lucius." Fear awoke in me. He was right. Nathan was right.

"What do you want from me?"

"I thought that part was obvious." He laughed loudly. His face turned serious. "I want your power."

"How are you playing on getting that?"

"By taking you and forcing you to everything I want you to." He took out a syringe and started walking towards me. I back up but only backed into another figure. They took a hold of me and forced me to my knees. He injected me.

" A little wolfsbane never hurt anybody. But it will keep you from contacting your boyfriend." He smiled evilly at me. The crowed started humming again.

The whole place around me started to look like black dots. The humming got louder and louder. My ears felt like it was going to burst. I wanted to scream but as soon as I opened my mouth nothing came out.

"There there love." Lucius picked me up. I couldn't move. I was immobilized.

"Let's take you to your knew home." He whispered in my ear.

In my mind I called out to Nathan. I hoped he could hear my calls. I hoped he would fine me. The pain got more from the mumbling. Louder and louder it got. Please make it stop. Please!! My inner voice was screaming now. Calling to Nathan.

"Nathan." I breathed out. Before I passed out in Lucius arms I saw a man walking towards me.

" Shame I liked you Lea." His voice was familiar. I looked at it.

It was Alex..

Chapter 9 - Rusv

I woke up in a dark room. Alex was standing in front of me holding another syringe. His eyes looked dark.

"Why?" I managed to get out.

"You weren't meant to be apart of this. But when the chief found out about you. He wanted you. Lea I am sorry. " he bent down. "I really liked you."

"Screw you." I spite out. He held my face in his hands.

"So beautiful, yet so stupid. But you will learn." He put the needle inside of me and started injecting me. " They all do."

I think I had thought of every possibility to escape. Non would work. Then it hit me. Nathan told me I have a wolf inside me. I just have to get in touch with her. But the more I kept trying the more I failed.

"Are you there?" I called. Nothing. I don't know how to get in touch with her. Maybe I am not a werewolf. Maybe I am human after all.

Alex entered again with a plate of food. And of course another needle. My heart started to pace. Whatever I was planning on doing I better do it now. 'Please please please help me' I pleaded in my head.

The next thing I know I jumped onto Alex, knocking the needle out of his hand. Something was different. I was on all fours on top of him. My skin was furry. It was gold. My wolf had come. I felt out of control, yet so much in control. Fear strike into the eyes of Alex. My wolf growled. She wanted flesh, she wanted blood. Before I could stop her she grabbed his neck inside her mouth. Ripping him open. Killing him in a instant. I felt myself turn back. I was covered in blood. My necklace was glowing. I grabbed the syringe and walked out the unlocked door and slowly crept upstairs. When I opened the door I was met by a huge living room. Filled with paintings and a red color scheme.

A couple of guys was walking and talking. My senses seemed to come alive. I could smell them. They smelled like mud.

"Yeah she's downstairs." The one said.

"I heard she was a seer." The other said.

"That's a myth. We all know the last seer died in the battle of the packs."

"Maybe a new one was born." They walked out. I saw my chance and started creeping towards the same door they left out of. There were massive fields and battle grounds outside. A lot of them were training. It looked like they were preparing for war. They were in both wolf from and human form. I saw the witches as well. Lucius was standing in the middle of them. They seemed to be doing some kind of ritual. All dressed in red. I had to get out of here.

I ran towards the gates. One guard saw me and I had to break his neck. With super speed I seemed to jump over the gate. My wolf wanted to come forward again and I let her. Transforming to my wolf form, I ran as fast as I could away from them. My speed increased when I heard a siren sound behind me. Suddenly I saw the black dots again. Nathan! I called before everything went completely black.

*****I woke up in a familiar bed. It was Nathans! He was sitting on the edge of the bed with his head in his hands.

"Nathan" my voice broke. He turned around.

"Lea!" He called out. He reached for me pulling me into a hug. He held me tight. "I was so worried."

"What happened?"

"You called for me. I found you far in the south, laying in the forest."

"My wolf came."

"I know. I saw her. A beautiful golden wolf." He cupped my face, pulling me into a kiss.

*****I was laying on top of his chest. Something felt off. Then I noticed a scar on my hand. I haven't seen that before. It was cut into a symbol.

"Nathan." I called out worried. Getting up straight.

"What is it?" He put his hand on my back.

"Look." I showed him. A frown spread on his face.

"We have to get you to the shaman now!" He ordered. ****The shaman studied the symbol. His face was emotionless. He got up and got a very old book. He brushed off the dust.

"Yes just as I thought. You were hexed."

"Hexed?"

"Yesss...hmm." He studied the book. "But not by a witch."

"The what!?" Nathan nearly screamed. Clearly angry.

"A fae. That's a fae's curse." He said calmly. "But its impossible. All the fae's were runned out of this country years ago. They wouldn't dare enter. If a werewolf saw them he would snap of her head."

"What does this symbol mean?"

"Its called a rusv. It means to break. Fae's used them to play pranks in werewolves. One of the biggest reasons the werewolves ran those tricksters out of town. It breaks the mates bond. Over time you wouldn't even remember your mate."

"How do we stop it?"

"I don't know. I would have to study more of Fae's magic. Luckily when my great grandfather killed the queen of fae's he took her spell book. I will study it and let you know whats the cure."

"Thank you." I couldn't imagine forgetting Nathan.

We walked out of the room and headed in the direction of Nathans men. They were training.

"Alpha Nathan." Two men came towards us. One elderly and the other a bit younger. A woman joined them.

"Alpha Nick, Alpha Rian." He addressed them. He looked at the woman. "Luna Agnes, I guess you are here in the name of your husband. How is doing?"

"He is starting to get better. May I ask why you summoned us."

"You are the strongest packs in the district. I need an alliance."

"And why do you need an alliance?" She raised her eyebrows.

"For war." ****I left them in the study to discuss their business. I was walking toward our bedroom. A omega woman who worked in the kitchen walked past me.

"Luna." She bowed her head. I smiled at her and nodded. "You seem to be glowing my queen."

"Thank you." I smiled and kept on walking. My head felt light. I grabbed the wall not to fall over. Then I saw a vision of my wolf. She was running in the forest. Behind her something was running. I looked closer. It was a pup. A red and golden pup. Then I knew it. I was pregnant.

Chapter 10 - Dear old Vincent

"How dare he disrespect me like that!" Nathan growled slamming his fist against the wall. It had been two months since I found out I was pregnant. Lucius hadn't tried anything again and we spent the better of the two months preparing for an all out war. I held my now showing baby bump and thought of the night I told Nathan.

"Nathan we have to talk." I was sitting on bed, pulling my knees to my chin.

"Yes my love." Nathan was now worried sitting beside me and putting a hand on my knee."

"I..I am pregnant." Nathan stood still for a moment. His face was in shock. Then a big smiled spread across it.

"I am going to be a dad?" His voice sounded happy.

"Yes."

"That amazing! How do you know."

I told him of my vision earlier.

"I don't understand how it can be a red and golden wolf. I thought the colors were given by the ranks."

"That true. But it can happen sometime that the genes can be mixed. It will most likely not happen with a omega and alpha. The seer gene is also very rare and doesn't get inherited that much. I guess we hit the jackpot then."

"Nathan....it's a boy."

"How do you know?"

"I just do."

"Well then he is going to be one hell of a strong alpha."

"I am the Alpha of one of the strongest packs and he speaks to me as if I am just a common mutt." Okay let me explain Nathans ranting:

He went to see Vincent for an alliance. Vincent is kind of the king of the vampires. Nathans beta advised him to get help from other supernatural entities, since Lucius has witches. The vampires control the city currently because of their ability to compel others. Even though the bite of the werewolf can kill a vampire, the werewolves fear them. The vampires control the leaders of the humans. Even though humans are weak, their numbers out weigh the supernatural and if they decide to turn on us, without knowing whats going on even, they can easily ruin us.

"Does he not remember the war of the packs!?"

The war of the packs I gathered was this huge war where all the pack fought for territory. A lot of innocent people got hurt, both supernatural and human. That is also how the shaman gathered my hex was created. Apparently one witch named Oliva had been abandoned by her coven as a baby. A fae found her and raised her as her own. After the faes was banished by the wolves she had found her coven again teacher them the magic of the faes. The hex doesn't really seem to effect me. Sure there are nights when I feel alone next to Nathan. But the more time we spend together, the stronger our bond grows. Just like our child. The shaman hasn't given up tho.

Back to the story. So basically Vincent told Nathan he doesn't want to get involved with werewolf businesses and that it shouldn't affect his city. Nathan saw that as a sign of disrespect.

"After this war is over I am going to get him next!"

"Just come to bed honey. We will figure this out tomorrow." Nathan stomped over to me. Clearly still pissed. He held me tight with one hand on my baby bump.

"I love you two." He sighed.

"We love you also."

The next morning I was trying to convince Nathan of coming on a walk with me through the gardens. Nathans beta Alec was waiting for us as we got to the bottom.

"Vincent is here." Was all he said as he walk to the study. We followed him. When we got inside my eyes was met by a beautiful man. He had dark brown hair with almost golden eyes. He starred at me and then looked at Nathan.

"A beautiful Luna you managed to get." Nathan growled at those words and put his hand around me protectively.

"Easy there old friend. I don't want your Luna. I mean she is pregnant for goodness sake." He walked closer. "Vincent." He greeted me placing a kiss at the back of my hand. Nathans grip increased.

"What do you want?" Nathan spat out.

"I got a proposal for you." Vincent made himself comfortable and poured himself a whisky.

" I am listening. "

"I will not help you fight the war. But my adviser advised me that I could use this to my advantage. I will give you something to stop the witches with. "

"In exchange for?"

"Let's just say a 'I owe you' this will be carried out by your entire pack. Even after the day you die. I can claim it at anytime."

"And what can you give me."

Vincent pulled out a dagger. It looked mystical.

"They say this dagger was forged by Merlin. You know the wizard from king Arthur and the round table. Well he used it to absorb Morgana, the evil witch's magic. They say if you can combine it with all the elements it can still absorb magic. But that would only last 48 hours until it is released back into them."

"Nathan." I whispered to him. "I don't trust him."

"Oh you don't have to trust my dear. But I got as far as I got for making the right deals to the rights people." He was looking at Nathan expectantly.

"Alpha I wouldn't....." Alec began.

"I'll do it." Nathan caught him off.

"Good then we are in a agreement." Vincent took out another dagger and cut his hand. Black blood came oozing out. He handed the dagger to Nathan, who did the same. They shacked bloody hands and nodded to each other. Vincent handed Nathan Merlin's dagger and smiled at me as he left.

A/N: I have reached 500 reads thank you so much. I will try my best to update everyday atleast one chapter❤❤

Chapter 11 - Betrothed.

All Nathans attention had been spend on this war. He ordered the shaman to stop looking for a way to break the hex ,but rather to spend is attention on getting the dagger ready. I wondered why Nathan was so fixated on this war. 'No one takes whats mine.' He growled when I asked him.

"But the shaman really? What if our bond breaks? Then all of this was for nothing.!"

"Do you feel our bond breaking?" He asked pulling me into a hug.

"No but maybe its a long term thing."

"I have a theory." He proclaimed.

"Yeah?"

"What if the hex only works when we are separated. I mean neither of us feel like our bond is growing weaker. In fact it grows stronger. Maybe that's why he kidnapped you. To separate us for as long as it takes the bond to be broken."

"That sounds about right."

A knock sounded at the door.

"Alpha." A young omega boy stepped in.

"Yes."

"You have a guest."

"Who?"

"She said her name was Mia." Nathans face went pale.

"Who's Mia?" I looked at him confused.

"A very old friend."

We headed into the study to great this Mia person. She was a tall red head and had good posture. She was dressed very formally.

"Great somebody is here to take my bags upstairs. " she looked irritated at me. She had a British accent.

"I am not..."

"Whatever just hurry." She rolled her eyes. I wanted to slap that bitches head of her shoulders. Nathan put a hand on my shoulder clearly seeing my anger.

"Mia what are you doing here?"

She moved her attention to him. "Nathan. It is good to see you." She smiled.

"You too Mia." He smiled back. "Let me introduce you. Lea this is Mia..she was uhh..my betrothed. Mia this Lea my mate and Luna."

Her eyes widened. I had a cheeky smirk on my lips. Wait! Betrothed? Like marry? Oh hell no.

"Luna." She bowed her head. "I am so sorry."

"Betrothed!?." I ignored her.

"It was many years ago. My father thought it would be a good idea. They were the second strongest pack and had good Alpha genes. He said our child would me more than powerful. But after the war they had to leave, because almost their whole pack was destroyed." He explained. I frowned. Clearly jealous.

"Now what are you doing here?"

"I need protection. Lucius influenced my entire pack I spend so long to rebuild. They are coming to kill me."

Nathan starred at her for a few seconds.

"Fine. I will protect you." What?

"No you won't." I know I was being petty but my wolf hates this woman.

"Lea can we talk. Nathan how about you go get us some tea." Nathan turned around and squeezed by shoulder before exiting the room.

Mia gestured me to take a seat. I did and so did she.

"Look I am sorry for before. I am used to looking down on Omega's."

"I am not an Omega." I said sharply.

"Oh seems like I can't get my foot out of my mouth." She chuckled. I gave no response.

"Nothing happened between me and Nathan. We were just friends. Close friends. We knew we were getting married one day so we made it our mission to get and know each other.

I must admit, I haven't met my mate yet and apart of me had hoped...but after Nathan told me I changed my mind. You deserve him and he deserves you. I need him now. I need you. So please I am asking you nicely reconsider."

I felt horrible for being mean to this woman. Her attentions was pure.

"Fine you can stay here." I sighed. "Sorry for my actions."

"Let's just start over okay?"

"I would love that." I smiled.

Shortly after that we were talking and making jokes when Nathan returned with a omega girl carrying our tea. It was the same girl who greeted me in the hall before I found out I was pregnant. She frowned when she saw Mia but left without saying a word.

"Lea we are watching romances and crying our eyes out tonight!" Mia exclaimed. "Its about time us girls got to know each other. I would have never thought this hard head would get a mate." We all laughed.

After Mia was shown her room, I saw that omega girl.

"Nathan go ahead I'll come in a little while." I headed in her direction.

"Hey." I greeted the girl.

"Is there a problem my Luna?"

"No it's just..when you saw Mia, you frowned. Why?"

"She looked like someone I saw a little while back."

"Who?"

"It was a woman who just got into town. I met a human friend of mine at a café down the street. This woman walked in. But she wasn't a werewolf.

Her Aroma was different, she had a werewolf aroma but I don't know something was very off. She seemed powerful. More powerful than a normal werewolf. Almost lycan powerful but it isn't her, they looked the same but the aroma was different."

I didn't like the sound of this.

"Luna. Can I tell you something?"

"Yeah?"

"I heard the reason Lucius uses witches is to steal the power from the werewolves he kills. There was a legend that they can do that. I don't know why the witches are helping him. I believe that woman does the same."

"Thank you...uhh.."

"Melina Luna."

"Melina. " I smiled. "You are very clever. I would like to have you at my side during this war."

"Thank you Luna." She bowed her head.

"Lea!" Mia called out opening her door. "Come on movie night!" She walked toward me and grabbed my arm. I turned my head back at Melina but she had already left.

Chapter 12 - Time for war

The scout has spotted Lucius men around our area and the time we all feared for has finally arrived. Everybody was reading themselves for war. The woman who can fight prepared themselves, while the other who wants to protect their children or with child like me were taken to a secure compound.

Mia joined us. She was a good fighter as well because of her Alpha genes but she chose to stay and protect us. Some of the omega also stayed with us, because they were to weak to fight. Nathan came to greet me and we were saying our final goodbyes. He held me tight against his chest, resting his head on my shoulder, with his face on the crook of my neck. I stood there taking in the scent of him for the final time.

"You better come back to me."

"I will beautiful. I promise I will."

"I refuse to raise my child without a father."

"You won't. Our baby will be raised to be a strong Alpha."

"Came back fast." I placed a kiss on his lips.

"I love you." He kissed my forehead.

"We love you too." We hugged again until he bent down on one knee.

"Hey buddy." He touched my very showing tummy know. "You better protect mommy while daddy's gone okay?" He kissed my belly stood up kissed me one last time and left with Alec walking next to him.

A lot of husbands, wife, boyfriends and girlfriends greeted their partners. Almost everybody was in tears. We knew this war was going to be intense. Everybody had months to prepare. The shaman came walking to me.

"Something around here seems to be blocking my magic." He warned. "You hadn't been having visions lately have you?"

"No not at all.".

" hmm. Well be careful something's not right okay." He walked with the rest of the men.

"Lea." Mia called behind me. I walked towards her.

"I think the people needs you they all seem pretty worried." I nodded my head and called everybody together.

"Listen. I know you are all worried about your loved ones. Your sons, daughters, husbands and wives are going out to battle and probably sacrificing their lives but remember they are doing this for you. For us. For our pack. That's probably the greatest honor a person can get. To give themselves for the lives of their loved ones. All of them are great fighters. We will win this war. We will rise above. That is a promise." They all started talking between themselves.

"Take care of your children and elders. They are the next generation after this war and will need the elders to guide them." I nodded my head and headed towards Melina. She looked upset.

"Whats wrong?"

"Nothing much Luna. I just found out I am pregnant but didn't get chance to tell my husband."

"I am sorry Melina. But he will return."

"That's good coming from a seer." She laughed.

I took a seat next to her and took out a book I managed to snatch from the library. A storm brewed and that made me even more worried. Fighting on a dark muddy field didn't sound very attractive.

Later that night a thunderstorm was on the happen. The scared children looked for protection from their mothers and fathers. Me and Mia were cuddled up in a blanket. We were just talking and trying to make jokes to calm our nerves. I started taking a liking towards Mia. She was actually nice and funny. You would not guess that from her perfectionism attitude.

"Luna someone was spotted outside the compound." A scout that was left to warn us came in.

"Stay here I'll go look." Mia said standing up, already showing her canines.

*****It had been over an hour and Mia still hadn't returned. I wanted to looked for her and called one of the guys who were meant to protect us to come with me.

We headed towards the area where the scout said the man had been spotted but no one was there. I walked further but still no one.

I spotted something. A body. I walked closer to see the body of the scout who had called us. This was all a trap!

A growling noise sounded near us and some howling. Both me and the guy stood ready for a fight. I couldn't change into my wolf form because I was so far pregnant but my protector did. He was a dark blue color. The color of the hunters.

The growling came near. I turned around because I heard something creak behind me. There was also nothing but pure darkness. Suddenly there was a thump noise behind me. I turned to see my protector laying on the floor bleeding. I rushed towards him but it was too late. There was no pulse.

I saw a wolf coming towards us. When it came close enough for me to see I could make out what color wolf it was.

A pitch black one.

It looked the same as Lucius's wolf just smaller in posture. The eyes was also different. It had less evil in them than Lucius but more hatred.

"I demand you show yourself."

The wolf only growled.

"If you are to be my maker I want to see who I am dealing with." I tried again.

"With pleasure." A female voice said from the wolf. Next thing I know the wolf transformed into a familiar redhead. It turned into...

Mia.

Chapter 13 - The shamans journal

A /N: yay! 1K reads thank you..this chapter is dedicated to ❤❤

"Mia why are you doing this, we protected you...wait your working with Lucius aren't you?"

"Of course I am not working with that fool! That was true what I told you. He did turn my pack against me but I killed them all. Including my mate.

I didn't came to you guys for protection. I came to get my husband back. The husband you stole." She spat.

"He is my mate." I said slowly.

"He was mine first. He promised to marry me and marry me he will."

"Over my dead body."

"Don't worry love, your body will be everything but alive when we are done here." She growled.

"Answer me one thing. How did you manage to hide your aroma?"

"You seriously don't think Lucius owns all the covens in the city. A witch is the easiest thing to be bought over."

"You clever bitch."

"Now if we are done talking here I would like to kill you already." She sprung forward and I landed on back. She was standing in her wolf form on top of me showing her canines. She came closer to my throat, knowing well I am not strong enough to defend myself. I felt tears escape my eyes.

Thump.

The weight on top of me was gone. I saw another wolf, greyish color snarling at Mia while she was lying on the ground. She got up ready to attack but fear struck in her. I turned my head to look at what she was looking at. A wolf army was standing there, of all colors and shapes. Mia ran into the forest.

The grey wolf turned back into human form. It was Lou my old trainer.

"Lou!" I ran forward and hugged him. "Thank you."

"No problem Luna." He hugged me back. "Lets head back okay?" We walked towards the people. They were completely unaware of the events that had just taken place. After my order one of the Omega's brought wine to me and Lou.

"Where Nathan?" I asked existed.

"Still on the battle field. We came back to let some of our men heal. It's a strategy. The first group goes in and does the most damage. Then they come back and let their wounds be treated to. Then the second and strongest group go forward and goes for the kill, while they are busy doing that we go back and double the impact."

"How is the war going?"

"It's hard. A lot of good men had fallen. Before we left I saw the shaman use the dagger. At least the witches powers had fallen but the most damage was already done. Nathan was searching for Lucius. He want blood."

"That's what I was afraid of." I looked around and saw the soldiers being treated. Some was just hugging their families. I really wish Nathan was here. Somehow I could feel our bond weakening with him not being here.

"Someone tried to hurt his mate, Lea, you must understand what that means. He would kill anyone to get his revenge. You would do the same if the roles were reversed."

"I know."

"We will leave first thing tomorrow morning. But first we got you something from the house." He pointed to the box I didn't even notice until now. I walked over the box and looked inside. It was filled with books from the library.

"I thought you might get a little lonely around here."

"Thank you Lou." I hugged him and started searching threw the books looking for something to break the curse. I cannot handle this anymore.

I found a book. It looked very old but it looked more like a journal than a book. When I opened it, it was in fact a journal and I started reading it.

From what I can make out it was the previous shamans journal. He lived in the times when the fae was still here. They irritated him. Apparently the most pranks was played on him because he also had magic. He said they feared him. He was very powerful. There were a lot of facts about the supernatural. Creatures I never heard of like Wendigos but also creature I never thought of like leprechauns. There was weaknesses and their specialty. Very interesting but I just couldn't keep my eyes open.

****I was standing alone on a mountain searching for them, my mate and my son, but I couldn't find them. I walked back down the mountain where Vincent was waiting for me. I got next to him in car.

"Time to forget Lea."

"Luna." I felt someone shaking me. I opened my eyes and saw Lou above me.

"Yes?"

"We are about to go thought you might want to say goodbye."

"Thanks Lou, I'll be right there." I smiled up at him. He nodded his head and went outside.

I sat up looking for the journal. Note to self: Get a journal diary, I need to write down everything. Maybe my son can also read about my life and adventures.

I walked outside and saw the men ready for action. Lou was informing them of the next tactics. I walked to Lou. After he was done, the men started marching. He hugged me.

"Be safe Luna. We will be back before you know it."

"You too Lou and take care of Nathan please?"

"Always my little Luna." He ran and joined his men.

I thought of my dream last night. It frightened me. I cannot lose them, I won't! I saw a piece of paper near me and grabbed a pen. I started writings down my dream, every single detail of what I can remember. After I was done I put the piece of paper in the old shamans journal and headed towards the rest of the people, they were either mourning about lost loved ones, either worried half to death about their mates or trying to calm down crying children.

All I could do know was take care of my people.

Chapter 14 - A fae's tale

After searching through the box for a second book, I notice there was a lot of journals that the old shaman wrote. I scanned through them to look for something about the faes. Found it!

'I was in my standing in the center of the moon feast. All supernatural entities gathering to honor the moon goddess. That was when I noticed her. A woman with a chocolate brown skin. She had curly black hair. Her curves fit perfectly into each other. A true beauty. Her amber wings glittered as the light of the fire reflected off it. When I got a look at her I could see a devilish glint in her face. She had done something!

Eric Williams ,our Alpha, had walked out of his house. His son Jason walking behind him, tripping at every second step. The child had just learned to walk. He seemed fixated on the woman. Marching towards her as Anger brewed in his face.

"What have you done!?" He shouted at her. All the joyful festivities had stopped now staring at her.

"Why, whatever do you mean?" She asked innocently.

"My wife barely recognizes me!" He shouted again.

"I told you don't mess with us Eric!"

"You have gone to far." Suddenly I felt a urge inside me to kill all the fae's. Erich had summoned his pack. All of them showed their canines, ready to attack. The fae's stood ready for action, but fear struck inside them. There was war. Some of the faes managed to escape but not all was so lucky. Even I against my will had killed some faes. They took the black haired beauty and threw her into a cage.'

"Is everything okay Luna?" Melina looked at me and my belly. We both knew my time was coming near.

"Yes thank you, Melina." I dived my head back into the journal.

'"What did you do?" I asked kneeling down next to her. Black orbs looked up at me.

"I took the little lady away from her hubby."

"How?"

"A hex." She smiled." It's called Rusv. It breaks the mates bond."

"Hows that possible?"

"Simple the more time the mates spend apart the more the bond weakens. That's how their bond had broken. The alpha spend so much time trying to make peace between the supernatural, that poor old wife spend all her time alone. The bond has broken."

"How do you reverse it?"

"Why would I tell you wolf?"

"I'll help you escape." She sat up straight.

"Why would you do that?"

"I'll do anything for my Alpha and my Luna."

"The reverse is simple. Open my cage and I'll tell you."

"Tell me first and then I'll open the cage. Fae's are tricksters I don't trust you."

"Fine." She groaned. "You will have to make them fall in love again. Then their bond would rebuild piece by piece." I opened the cage and let the woman out. She walked out slowly and looked at her surroundings. Then she placed a tiny kiss on my lips and whispered in my ear.

"May we meet again."'

I knew this distance between me and Nathan wasn't good. The sooner he gets back the sooner we can fix this. I miss him so much.

I looked through more of the journals when I saw Nathans name.

'The young Alpha is strong but not very wise. Because of his fathers bitterness after he lost his mate, after I failed my mission, Eric took out all of his frustrations on Jason. Jason didn't grow up to be much different. He had a lovely Luna, who knew her duties. I don't think Love played a huge factor. His poor son, Nathan, and daughter, Anne had suffered the consequences.

This will be my last journal. My second in line has come of age and it is time for him to write his own stories. I hope these journals will guide him and he will be a great shaman to Nathan when he becomes Alpha.

To our next Alpha, I beg you not to repeat the actions of your father and grandfather. I heard of a vision from the last seer. She had said that the next Alpha son would be one of a unique breed. Difficult times will arise, but stay strong you must the father beyond fathers. Your son will change the course of the supernatural. She said he would have a unique bond with the vampires and that would guide him in the right direction. I beg you Alpha take care of him. Forever.

To our next Luna. Don't follow your mates example. They did not build their foundation on love but rather strategy. You must build him because he suffered a lot. Do not abandon him. He needs love, because he never had had any for himself.

And finally to the next shaman: Use these guides I beg you. You must take care of our pack but I know in all my heart that you would be a worthy a successor. Now I am off to find the love that had gotten away. A fae who I had mentioned that had captured my heart. Until we meet again.

Linkin.'

Wow. I felt like I was intruding but I couldn't help but read that. I finally know how to stop the hex. I have to make sure that me and Nathan never has stop spend a long time apart after this again. And if he comes back I will not allow that.

A/N: I won't be updating the next three days probably because I have to go see a doctor in another town....struggles of living in a small town.

Chapter 15 - The warriors return

One by one the men who fought in the war was beginning to return. All of them seemed pretty broken up and hurt. I saw Lou and ran towards him.

"Did we win?" His eyes looked sad.

"Yes."

"Then whats the problem?"

"We can't find Nathan?"

"What do you mean you can't find him?"

"I mean he is gone. He can't find him. One moment he was fighting next to us, the next he was gone."

"And Lucius?"

"He is dead. The beta, Alec killed him."

"Then who took Nathan!?"

"We were ambushed. Mia showed up with some of her followers. Mostly witches. The daggers energy had worn off and the witches got their power back but they didn't attack they just stood their. The next thing we knew, Nathan was missing."

"Mia came." I gritted threw my teeth.

"Sorry Luna but we will send our best trackers to track him down I promise."

A\N: Yes I know you hate me for not letting Nathan return yet but sadly I am working with a plan.

"Where's Alec?"

"Down with the rest of the soldiers, making sure there arrant severe wounds or foul play that was used."

"Okay."

I rushed over toward Alec. He was in fact where Lou said he was.

"Alec." I called. He ignored me flatly.

"Alec?" I tried again. He walked over towards the next soldier. I followed.

"Alec as your Luna I command you answer me."

"You are not my Luna!" He finally answered.

"What's going on with you Alec?" My eyes was wide with shock.

"This is all your fault. You started this war. You let these men get hurt. It's because of you that our Alpha is missing. You, you, you!"

"Alec you know...."

"And as acting Alpha, my first order will be to revoke you of your Luna duties."

"You can't do that!"

"Yes I can and I am. If you were born in this pack you would've known this! And that's exactly my point, you are an outsider in this pack throwing your weight around just because your mate happens to the Alpha. If you weren't to Nathan you wouldn't give two craps about us.

The council would agree with me, they aren't very fond of you either. But if you want to make this official we can always go to them. From now on and not a second further you will no longer be Luna of this clan.

You can still use the Alpha bedroom, if Nathan isn't to return you will be kicked out. You can work your way up into the pack, until your son and the next Alpha comes of age. He will them decide what your fate is in the future.

You will see him three time a day after he is born. To breastfeed and that's it. You will not have contact with or influence him. The elder mothers in the pack will raise him and teach him to be a good Alpha."

Tears stung in my eyes. How could he, Nathan's beta and best friend do this to me? To him? I didn't know the pack hated me so much.

"Over my dead body." I answered coldly and walked off.

"Luna are you alright?" Melina called out.

"I am no longer your Luna."

"What do you mean?"

"Alec revoked me of my Luna duties."

"How could he do that? It's for the council to decide."

"Oh trust me the council would agree."

"I am sorry Luna. I will speak to my husband, this must be a misunderstanding."

I was taken back by her words. Husband?

"Alec is your husband?"

"Yes Luna. We keep it quiet because he is second in command and I am a Omega but you cannot deny the mates pull."

"No." I said understanding. "Leave it, I don't want problems between you and your husband. I will sort out this myself and just pray that Nathan will be found quickly. At least before the birth of his firstborn son." I sighed.

"We all hope so Luna. Even Alec. He is more of a fighter than a leader. That's why he makes such stupid mistakes, like taking away the packs mother. Without you, we who were left over wouldn't have made it. Thank you Luna!" She bowed her head.

"No problem." I smiled. "Just don't call me Luna in front of your husband."

"Oh I think I can handle him." We both laughed.

I walked back into the compound to gather all my stuff. I am stealing all the journal of the old shaman and everything I can find about the history of this pack and his people. Something inside me tells me this is going to be a long war until my love returns and I am making sure I am winning this for my family. I stroked my belly and had a quick vision of my sons wolf and mine running threw the forest happily playing. There was a mans presents with us. Who I couldn't really make out.

A young girl came towards me. She was about 13 or 14.

"Thank you Luna."

"No problem. My I ask why you are thanking me?"

"My grandmother was heart broken when she found out, both my father and her husband went off to the war. She wanted to die. After you speech she kept hope that they both would return. And so both of the men did indeed return. You are a marvellous Luna!" She hugged me and I hugged back.

See this right here is why we will be fighting for our position as Luna. Alec wants a war, I say we give it to him. My wolf spoke to me and I agreed with her.

Chapter 16 - The baby is coming

"Ahhhh!" I screamed. My face full of sweat and tears. Who ever said giving birth was easy will have their head ripped from their neck from me. If it wasn't my wolf giving strength to me, I wouldn't have survived. Nathan still hasn't returned and every time we send out a tracker they either don't return or return injured.

Alec is enjoying his role as the new Alpha too much to even care about finding Nathan. Just wait till Nathan returns we will cut Alec into pieces slowly and....sorry about us being so aggressive, it's the childbirth, the stress of my mate, the fact that I don't know what will happen to me after my son is born.

It was already 3 hours I was laying here in labour. Thankfully this was a regular hospital with regular people. I kind of miss this old life of mine. I had to give up teaching after this whole Lucius story. I really wasn't in the mood to get kidnapped again by one of my former coworkers, but all these people that are rushing around remind me of my childhood. My mom used to be a nurse or rather my foster mother. I really didn't know my parents. They died when I was still a child, that explains me not knowing I was a wolf.

As for the regular hospital, you are probably wondering why I a werewolf is giving birth to a werewolf baby between all the humans. Well as I learned apparently the werewolf only turns after the age of 16 or when they had killed their first person. So besides the threat of me turning full canine on these people, everything was going to be okay.

Besides the pack house might have a healer but I don't trust anybody from the pack with my child. Especially not with Alec and the council controlling everything around there.

"Come on push." The doctor said calmly.

What the f- do you think I have been doing you idiot!

Sorry like I said giving birth was not easy.

"We are almost done. Just one final..." He was interrupted by a baby crying. After cutting the umbilical cord and sort of cleaning the baby, they hadn't him to me. I was starring at pure joy at my son. He was beautiful. I believe that every mother says that of their young ones but he, he was truly amazing. I immediately felt unexplainable love and protection towards this baby. He was mine and I would give my life just to make sure that he was safe. How I wish Nathan was here.

"Whats his name?" One of the nurses asked looking at the both of us.

"Aden" was all I said. I remembered that Nathan once told me if he was ever to have a son he would name him Aden. Why? I don't know but when Nathan returns I would find out for sure.

I decided that after I get out of this hospital I and my son would make a run for it. I would not let them take my boy away from me. We will go and find my mate ourselves. Screw the pack! Their loyalty only lies with their ranks, not their own opinions.

While busy lying there and resting a bunch of men marched in. Some I recognized as hunters from the pack. They seemed to go unnoticed by the humans even though they are pretty obvious!

"What do you want?" I asked sharply.

They didn't answer, all they did was walk over towards my son. I knew what they were going to do.

"No!" I screamed and pushed myself forward. Even though I am weak I still had power to push the closest one away. The rest of the guys came to hold me down. I was fighting with everything inside of me. They cannot take my son. The door opened, one of the nurses came in.

"Oh I am sorry. I didn't know you had company." Was all she said with a smile before existing.

The men started packing my bags. The one that I pushed away was now holding my son. They all helped me into the car sitting tightly next to me. My son was in another car with the other man. They are literally separating us. I will kill them all!

Tears were burning in my eyes. How can one pack be so kind the one day and so cruel the next. Why are the taking a son away from his own mother!

We drove into the pack house. They again took me like one of their prisoners and lead me upstairs to a bedroom. It was not our bedroom. All of them exited accept one guy.

"I will kill you all." I warned. My canines was clear as hell by now. My breathing was heavy. I was furious!

"When you have calmed down, the council would like to speak to you and your duties in the pack from now on." He existed the room and I heard the door get locked behind him.

I will get my son back and I will kill each and everyone of these bastards even if I have to kill myself in the progress. My wolf was going crazy. She was brawling a war inside of me. There was going to be hell fire.

Chapter 17 - The council

The door unlocked. I never ate the food they gave me, didn't wash my face so it was full of tear and eyeliner marks. I just sat on the floor and let my head rest on the bed. Fighting didn't help. After I have destroyed the entire room and spent the entire day scratching up the door and everything around me, no one came. They just ignored me and kept me locked up. Even if it meant that I would kill myself. They didn't care.

I turned into my wolf a couple of times, but somehow I wasn't strong enough to break the door.

Stepping inside was Alec, not alone tho but with other men as well. I was ready to launch myself towards him but the men pinned me down.

"The council wants to see you." They took me downstairs towards the car.

We drove for hours like it seemed to me, until we finally stopped next to a big building. The men took me towards the building with Alec walking in front.

When we entered there was about 16 people sitting in a crescent moon position. In front of them was huge tables filled with books and papers.

They were all dressed pretty formal. In the middle of the group a guy was sitting slightly higher than the rest. I am guessing he speaks for the council.

What I have learned through my studies, the council is linked through mind speak. All the voices are rambled into the head of the speaker. He then combines them and judges them and then he makes his final judgement.

The council is only really seen when a werewolf does something really bad or when a important choice is made regarding the pack.

"Lea Jackson sit down." The guy in the middle commanded. I obeyed and sat down in the seat in the middle. I saw Lou coming from a door behind them, also dressed neatly in a suit. He came to stood beside me.

"You are a rough who smuggled herself into the head of an Alpha."

"That is not...." Lou placed his hand on my shoulder, telling me to keep quiet.

"Your pack doesn't accept you as Luna anymore, therefore you have two choices." He remained silent, as if he was listening to the voices speak.

"You will either stay in the pack, but only as a Omega. You will serve the Beta, and when your son comes of age, you will serve him." He remained silent once again.

"Your second choice will be to leave the pack. If you were to return then we will immediately kill you, you will not see your son ever again."

"What if I choose to stay, when will I see my son."

"Until he has come of age you will never see him. Only to breastfeed as Alec has ordered you once before.

You are now welcome to consult with your elder. We will resume in 15 minutes."They stood up and started walking towards the door.

"Lou." I stood up and hugged him. "At least someone's on my side."

"Are you okay Lea?" He looked me into my eyes.

"I don't know. I don't know what to do." I looked down.

"I say you stay. At least you get to see your son and when he comes of age he will choice you to guide him. "

I thought for a moment.

"No." I stood firm. "I will not allow them to bully me into something. I will leave and when I return, I will be strong. I will take back my son and I will find my mate."

"Lea, please think about what you are saying. This will be hard. We are one of the strongest packs. This isn't a very wise..."

The council returned. They took their seats and the room fell silent.

"Have you decided Lea Jackson?" The speaker spoke and broke the silence.

"Yes." I stood firm but my entire body was shaking inside. "I will leave the pack." The entire room burst into people talking and gasps from both the council members and others. I think they didn't suspect that response.

"Lea think about this!" Lou tried again.

"Quiet!" The speaker ordered. "Lea Jackson is this your final decision?"

"Yes." Was all I said. Everybody in the room looked shocked.

"Very well, you will leave the pack never to return."

"Oh no I will return. One day is one day."

"Don't make threats you cannot keep Jackson." Alec said from the side.

"I can and will keep it Alec." I spat out.

"You may leave Lea." The speaker commanded.

*****

For the first time in forever I sat in a regular human bar. I was burring my sorrows in alcohol. I felt a presents come and sit next to me. I looked up and saw the one and only king of the vampires. Vincent.

Chapter 18 - The maze

Nathans POV:

For three days I was running around in the middle of nowhere. I have never seen this place in my life. It seems like I have been running in circles the whole time. The last thing I remembered was seeing Lucius on the battle field. I was on my way to rip that son of a bitch to pieces, when everything around me went black suddenly.

And now for the first time in the days I see my capturer. Mia. She stood in front of me in a pure white silk dress. The wind was blowing heavy. They called this the witches wind. I have heard of it before.

"Why Mia?"

"You and I were meant to be together, don't you see that Nathan?"

"I love her and you know it."

"You love me! And after my hex has completed you will see that."

"Your hex?"

"You know nothing about me Nathan. Did you really think I left because of the war. Our marriage would have protected my family! No I left because my daddy Alpha found out he wasn't my daddy. I was a bastard. My real daddy was a powerful warlock. How do you think I managed to get the witches on my side."

"And Lucius?"

"Lucius was a pawn in my game. He played exactly like I wanted him too. Fools mind. Thought he can convince my witches to join him by giving them power."

"What are you going to do to me?"

"I am keeping you here. At least until the hex is completed. Then I will make you see how much you love me." She stepped forward towards me. I wanted to grab her but she was gone in a instant.

"Not even dating yet and you are already getting touchy." A voice said behind me. I turned to see Mia behind me.

"I will never forget her!"

"Oh but you will." And with that she was gone.

****Months have passed. My physical body was getting treated very well. I noticed that every time they do something to my body in real life it appears on this projection. My beard gets shaved regularly. I am bathed and all the other necessaries.

I was lying in the hut I had build myself. I was still walking in circles and still haven't found a way out.

"Nathan" I heard almost a whisper of a male voice. I sat up.

"Nathan!" It was there again but I still couldn't see anything. I walked out of the hut. I saw a glowing white circle in middle of the field.

"Go inside it."

"Who are you?"

"Go inside quickly. We don't have a lot of time before the witch wolf returns."

I had no choice, I had to trust the voice. I walked towards the white circle and everything went white in front of me.

Suddenly I was in a room. It was a prison like room. In the room with me was a old man and a woman. The woman was a fae you could clearly see that. The man looked familiar but I couldn't but my finger on it.

"You finally awoke Nathan." The man spoke.

"Who are you? Where am I?"

"You clearly don't remember me." He sighed. "I was your fathers shaman. I left to find my love..." He looked at the woman. "And shortly after I found her, we ran into the wolf witch. She seemed nice at first, wanted our protection but sadly after we learned of her plan with you, well we ended up here.

We spent months trying to revive you, but the witches power was too strong. She seemed to be out for a little while so we took our chance."

"Where am I?"

"A prison inside one of her compounds. We move every week to a new one. With you awake we have a good chance of escaping."

"How many months has it been?"

"Plenty. We met a merchant along the way, he sang praises of the new Alpha that was born. I imagine that is your son."

"Do you know his name?"

"Aden." The woman finally spoke.

I smiled. She remembered.

"And Lea?"

"She left the pack." The man sighed. "Was forced out by your beta and the council."

"Where is she now?"

"Nobody knows."

I felt anger boil inside me. I was going to kill Mia by ripping her to pieces and then I was going to deal with Alec.

Chapter 19 - Meeting the Vampire king.

L ea's Pov:

"So I heard you had a tough couple of days love." Vincent said beside me.

"Whats it to you?" I said harshly not in the mood.

"Hey I am not the bad guy. I think you currently need all the friends you can get." He said lifting his hands up in the air.

"Sorry what do you want?" I sarcastically tried to say nicely. He let out a deep chuckle taking another sip of his whiskey.

"I like you. You are feisty."

I patiently waited for him to continue.

"I have a preposition for you."

"That is?"

"You should become my queen."

"What?!"

"You heard my pretty."

"Why the hell would I do that?"

"Because it means you can get your son back."

"Explain?"

"I still have that little deal with your...uh..former pack. I could simply ask for the young baby and sadly for them they would have to give it up. Beside I am the vampire king! I control almost all the supernatural entities and the humans included. They fear me. They would not deny me what I ask for."

"And what do you get out of this deal?"

"Why a beautiful queen of course."

"Vincent." I said irritated.

"That my little bird is my reasons."

"I will not do it if I don't get answers."

"Some prophecy about the child being the strongest werewolf ever lived. I would like to have someone like that on my side. I am a clever man beautiful." He took another sip. "And what better way to control a man than through his mother."

"If I didn't allow another pack to control me why on earth would I allow you."

"You see that's the thing. You would be free to do as you please. You and your son will live in my house. He will grow up in my house. We can be friends, that is if you can resist my charms. I don't believe in love so wooing you isn't a option. We are allies. I plan on gaining your loyalty and through that your sons."

"And that's all? No extra terms?"

He shook his head. "Nothing I can think of wolf."

"And if I decide to go find Nathan?"

"He is probably dead by now." He said and I winced. I would've felt it if he had died, I know it. "But if that is your wish my love, than sure. Just be patient at first, it will take time to get the boy back. Packs don't kindly give up their future alpha."

"I guess we got a deal then." I was impulsive lately, I meant just stick to it, I have gotten this far already.

"Great." He bumped his glass against mine. "I will let the news travel that I have found my queen. Then we can start preparing the arrival of your son." He stood from his stool, downed the last of the glass and took out money to pay for it.

"Vincent." I called before he left. He looked at me. "Thank you." He smirked at me.

"No problem sweetheart'

Chapter 20 - The red wolf

I was sitting in my new room, when I heard a knock on the door.

"Come in." Vincent stepped in. I got to know him a little better these last couple of days. He is actually a true gentlemen, never tried to overstep his boundaries. Also very clever, he has so many strategies worked out, I stepped into his office once. It was filled with books, fiction and nonfiction, next to his desk he has a whiteboard filled with scribbles I could not understand. I knew he wasn't from around here but where he was from, I do not know.

"Yes?"

"Come it's time."

"Time for?" He stepped out before answering. It couldn't be our ceremony. Yes becoming the queen of vampires requires some sort of ceremony, almost like a wedding. I followed Vincent down stairs. When I reached the bottom I stopped dead in my tracks. My wolf filled with anger.

In front of me stood Alec and some of his fighters. He looked pissed.

"So you decided to fuck your why into another position of power." He spat.

"But the vampires? How low can you go Lea?"

"Watch it wolfie. I could easily rip your neck off, or better yet make you do it yourself." Vincent spoke.

"What are they doing here?" Beyond pissed was my expression.

"I thought you wanted your son, little bird?"

"If you think we are going to hand our Alpha...." Nathan begin but was interrupted by a laughing Vincent.

"Now now wolf, you see your Alpha made a deal with, I can get whatever I want, and what I want is that baby. Now you got two choices. One you give me the baby. Two I rip the head of every single member of your pack, including you, and take the baby." He smirked. "So what will it be."

Alec sighed and nodded his head. Melina came walking in with my son in her arms.

"We will came back for that child." Alec said as Melina handed the baby over to me. I mouthed a thank you and felt tears in my eyes as I held my baby boy. The wolf pack left and I was left standing alone with my king to be.

"Thank you." I looked up at him with a smile.

"Hey, a deal is a deal." He smirked at me. I stepped closer to him, the distance between us was very small. I stood on my toes, realising how tall he actually is, and placed a small kiss on his cheek. He looked at me shocked and then his expression changed into something else, I don't know what really. Lust?

"I have something to show you." He said shaking it off.

"Yeah?"

"Come."

We walked in silence into a room I had not visited before. He opened the doors and it looked like an art studio.

"I...I did some research on your history, apparently you wanted to go to art school when you were done with school but teaching called harder. So I made my people get some supplies and make you a studio."

"Oh Vincent I don't know what to say."

"I thought I might as well make the house pleasant for you since you will be staying here for a while. Missy." He called and a elderly woman stepped in. "Please take the baby and settle him into the nursery." She nodded and took my child from me.

"I will leave you to it then." Vincent stepped back and closed the doors while walking out.

I walked over to the canvas, hold a brush. Hmmm. My wolf was screaming at something to draw but I couldn't put my finger on it. I dabbed my brush in the red paint and as soon as my brush hit the canvas everything around me went white suddenly.

I woke on hard wooden floor. I rubbed my eyes to get a better view while sitting up. I was still in the studio. Everywhere around me papers were scattered. What happened?

I decided to examine the paper. On every single paper the same thing was drawn. A red wolf.

This was some kind of vision, of what I don't know, but the red wolf could only mean one thing. Nathan. He is still out there and this confirms he is still alive!

I haven't thought about him since I moved into Vincent house. I guess I was too preoccupied with other things, like getting my son back. I could feel our bond is very weak, hardly even there. Guilt crept over my entire body, how could I have allowed this to happen? I could I forget my one true love?

I rushed out of the room and into my child's nursery. Our child. He lied sound asleep. So innocent, not a worry in the world. Now I was sad that this child never met his father and at the rate things are going now, probably never will. Tears were stinging in my eyes. Today was a day of tears it seems.

"Miss Jackson." I heard a whisper behind me. I turned to see a man around my age. He was very handsome and lean.

"Yes?"

"The master would like to know if you would be joining for dinner. Apparently it is a very special occasion." He smiled at me knowingly.

"No not tonight." I looked down. What are you going to do cry yourself to sleep?

The man gave a nod and started to leave.

"What!" I whisper yelled after him. He stopped in his tracks and looked at me.

"I will join your master for dinner."

"Very well." He nodded. "Your attire is already laid out on your bed." He now officially left.

My what?

Chapter 21- The return

I looked at the dress that was lied out for me. It was a short black lace dress. Next to it equally lacy lingerie. This was obviously Vincent's idea. I dressed obediently because I knew that Vincent was not one to be messed with.

After getting dressed I headed towards the dining room, I almost got lost because this place was huge. Vincent was already sat at the table. His expression changed when he saw me and immediately he stood up, pulling out the chair for me. I sat and he shifted the seat in for me. Chivalry ain't dead ladies.

"You look beautiful." He starred at me. I just smiled in response.

"I invited a guest over." I gave him a confused look. He nodded his head towards the door. My heart swelled when I saw who entered. Anne and Jason cautiously walked inside. I immediately stood up and pulled Anne into a tight embrace. It was so good to see her. My wolf jumped at the familiar scent of my mate. It was the first time my wolf gave reaction, all this because family came to visit.

"Please sit down." Vincent called.

Anne and Jason took their seats and looked around.

"A vampires castle looks a hell lot better than the pack house." Jason stated.

"I have a century advantage to create the house." Vincent stated. That made me wonder how old Vincent really is. I know werewolves can age up to 200 and still look between 20 and 50 but vampire they can live up to a thousand years, maybe even more. I don't know much of vampires.

"How have you been Anne?"

"Fine dear." She smiled "The school is quiet without you, even John misses you." We laughed.

"I miss it too. My life was so normal back than." My heart felt sad. I really wanted that life back. Even without your mate? I could never go back to normal. Vincent sensed my sadness and grabbed my hand to comfort me. Anne frowned eyes fixates on our hands.

After dinner the boys left, something about ancient armor and king Arthur and I don't know. Anne looked deep in thought. I lead her to the fireplace, both of us with wine glasses in our hands. Mine was nearly finished, while Anne's looked like she hardly touched hers.

"Geez I missed wine." I said downing the last of my glass.

"Where is the little one?" Anne seemed to snap out of her daze.

"He is asleep." I smiled.

"Lea, do you trust him?"

"Trust who?"

"Vincent."

"I don't know. Maybe?"

"I wouldn't if I was you." Her expression was hard.

"Why?"

"I heard rumors."

"What type of rumors?"

"Bad ones."

"Explain."

"Apparently Vincent was creating hybrids from rouges, he somehow manages to mix his blood and theirs. If this is true. Lea your son is one of the strongest werewolves to exists. If he created the hybrid and raise that boy as his own son, imagine the power he will have. And with Vincent power is everything."

Anger rose within me. I am so going to kill him later.

"Trust me Anne, I won't allow that." I gritted through my teeth.

"Just be careful Lea, that's all I am asking. I don't want anything to happen to my brothers son."

"And nothing will."

Vincent and Jason came in laughing and chatting as if they were the best of pals. I gave Vincent a cold stare and he gave me a later look.

We said our goodbyes and I bolted straight to Vincents room.

"Whats going love?" Vincent joined me, starting to undress. I was about to answer but his abs got my attention. I drew my eyes away and looked him straight in his eyes.

"You want to use my son as a hybrid freak to gain power." I bluntly stated. He looked at me shocked.

"Excuse me?"

"Oh please I know of you whole hybrid army thing."

"They are volunteers and there was no success as if yet." He stated already bored.

"And if you succeed?"

"I will not use a infant! What kind of monster do you think I am." I frowned. He walked over to me trying to calm himself.

"Look, I have a plan with your son yes, but turning him into some hybrid isn't included okay?" Before I could answer his lips crashed into mine. I was took back by the moment. His hand guided itself towards my butt, squeezing it lightly. I gasped. He too the opportunity to enter my mouth. I couldn't help it. I just wanted to feel normal again, so I kissed him back.

*****I woke up with a scent filling my nose. Mate! It can't be. I looked over at Vincent, he was sound asleep. I quietly got up and got up following the scent. I headed into the nearby forest. When I reached my destination I saw a man stand next to an much older guy and woman. Mate!

That can't be Nathan! He doesn't look anything like him. I mean Nathan looks like.....uh...like...I can't remember. The hex! It worked, well almost.

"Lea?" The man spoke. Butterflies rose in my stomach.

"Nathan?" I said with a nod. He smiled and headed over to me , but stopped directly in front of me, unsure of what to do. I pulled him into a hug, taking in his scent. Something felt slightly off. I pulled away.

"Whose this?" I pointed to the other two.

"Uh this is John and that Isabella, he used to be my fathers shaman." Guild crept in my body knowing I read that man's journal.

"Luna." They nodded.

"I...err...am no longer Luna." I nervously rubbed my arm.

"What?" Nathan asked looking slightly angry.

"I'll explain it later lets go inside please?"

"Inside to Vincent house?" Nathan frowned. I suddenly remembered my night with Vincent and my promise to me his queen. Shit!

"Like I said I will explain now let's....."

"Lea?" I spun around to see Vincent behind us. Double shit.

Chapter 22 - You have a choice

A smirk played on Vincent lips, if it was real or forced that I did not know.

"Nathan. Old friend, welcome home." Nathan frowned. Instead of answering, Nathan stepped forward and shake hands with Vincent.

"Thank you more taking care of my mate." Nathan said fiercely like an Alpha should. The word 'mate' stung inside me like a bee.

"No problem, but please come inside, you got a lot of catching up to do." Vincent winked at me. The old shaman and fae followed Vincent inside, it was only me and Nathan left standing.

"Do you want to see your son?" I asked nervously as if talking to a stranger.

"I would love that." He gave me a warm smile. He put his hand on the bottom of my back and lead my inside. Something of his touch, it gave a sort of electric pulse running over me. I shivered.

"You okay?" Nathan asked. I just nodded in response.

"I heard you named our son, Aden." He tried to spike up conversation.

"Yeah, you wanted that."

"I remember." And just like that the conversation went dead. We walked in silence the rest of the way. When we got inside Vincent left for his study, probably to replan his strategy since things changed, he also gestured one of the human servant he compelled to take the rest up to their rooms. I showed Nathan the way to the Nursery. When we got inside Nathan froze, he kept starring down at Aden.

"You can pick up you know?" I reassured him. He took the baby in his arms, something almost like a tear formed in his eyes.

"Hey there young one." He spoke softly.

"I will be leaving you two then, my room is just across the hall." After I left Nathan and Aden I bolted to Vincent study.

He sat at his desk, deeply concentrating on the papers he had in front him.

"Vincent." I called to get his attention. He looked up, his face was emotionless.

"Are you okay?" He nodded and looked back down at the paperwork, it seemed as if he was trying to calm himself.

"Vincent talk to me." He slammed his pen down, clenching his jaw. He rubbed his eyes and looked up at me.

"What can I say, I let my guard down and now all my plans at scattered because of it."

"What plans?"

"Nothing that matter now."

"What...what about our deal? The whole being queen thing?"

Vincent sighed. "Well that dear Lea, is simply your choice. I can't force you to love me now can I?"

"That's the thing." I felt tears burn in my eyes. "I currently feel more for you, than Nathan. I hardly know him!"

"It is all because of the curse. In time your feelings will return."

"And if I choose to stay with you?"

"We both know you won't, the bond is already being reestablished. The mate pull will call you."

Tears stung in my eyes, he spent the night with me and it didn't mean a single thing. He wouldn't even fight for me and here I thought he cared about me.

"Nathan may never know. About us I mean."

"I won't be the one who tells him, sweetheart."

I turned and opened the door.

"One last thing." I turned to face Vincent.

"I made a deal with the pack remember. The child, it stays with me."

"What!?"

"That will be all." He dismissed me with his hand. Anger boiled inside me as I slammed the door shut. I walked to my room, only to find Nathan sitting on my bed, he stood up as soon as he saw me.

"You seemed distressed." He walked closer to me.

"It's nothing, just some old drama." He took his hand and put it on my cheek. Warms and lightning filled my body.

"Do you need something?"

"Yes." He removed his hand and shifted on his feet nervously. "I don't really know how to explain it but uhmm I felt like I needed to be near you, you understand?"

"Yeah I understand, I feel it too, it's the mates pull."

"Do...do you mind if I sleep here tonight?" That question blew me away. My wolf came alive. I could feel her stir. How can I deny my mate to sleep with me, even if he felt like a complete stranger. Apart of me screamed to let him in, another part felt guilt over my actions with Vincent. A man who didn't even care about me one single bit. I was just a pawn in his pathetic plan to conquer the world, or whatever. A man who wanted to take my child away from me.

"Yes you may sleep next to me." I said in defeat. The best I could do is try to recover the mates bond and forget that bloodsucking leach.

He grinned deeply and started removing his shirt and pants.

"What...what are you doing?"

"This is how I always sleep beautiful." Memories flashed back to our nights together, that was in fact how he slept. I also remembered the nickname he gave me when we met. Beautiful.

I entered the closet and dressed in a wide T-shirt and panties, I guess Nathan has saw me in less so what does it really matter right? When I existed the closet, Nathan was already laying on his side the bed which he claimed before I got a chance, I remembered his arrogance which I both loved and hated. I entered the bed next to him, we weren't touching but it felt intimate. I allowed sleep to take over my body and help me temporary forget.

******Okay so I am curious, who do you like more Nathan or Vincent? And who would be better match?

Let me know!!

Also thank you I am #181 in werewolf and almost have 10K readers thank you and love you guys.

Chapter 23 - The truth shall set you free

A /N: Okayy so I still wanna know who fits best with Lea..Nathan or Vincent?? Let me know. Thanks!!

Somehow through the night I crept into Nathans arms, because when I woke up, my head was on top of his hard chest and one leg slung over him. I slowly and carefully sneaked away from me and headed towards the shower.

The warm water grazing my skin was all I needed from this mess. I didn't want to leave, I just wanted to stay in this shower forever. I quickly got dressed upset for leaving the warm comfort of that shower. I dressed in a white tank top and light skinny jeans. When I entered the room again Nathan had left. A part of me was upset and another glad I didn't have to face the awkwardness yet.

The kitchen was full when I entered. Anna and Jason had come to great her brother. Along with John, my former student and Nathans brother. I have to admit, I was glad to see the little brat. He winked at me.

"Glad to see my teacher is alive, maybe she can return and then the school can finally have a little bit of beauty." Great a 16 year old flirting with me.

At the end of the table other John (The old shaman) and Isabella was sitting, looking all happy and in love. In the end of his last journal he mentioned that he went out in search of his one true love, I guess he found her. Who would've thought that a fae who was held captive, could capture a shamans heart in a matter of seconds. Nathan entered, his eyes fell on mine and he smiled at me. I smiled back.

"Morning beautiful." He greeted lying on the wall.

"Morning." I said and broke eye contact, grabbing a bowl and filling it with fruit salad. Vincent didn't join us for breakfast. I wondered if he was busy fixing his errors.

"So tell me what I missed." Nathan asked. The room fell silent. Anne and I gave each other a look.

"Well you missed the big game. We almost won but that freaking ref doesn't know how to blow a whistle." Jason said stuffing his mouth with scrambled eggs. We all gave him that please shut up look.

"You missed your pack stripping me of my rank." I finally and bluntly said.

"Why would they do that?" He looked me dead in they eyes, I felt like he was searching all my secrets. About him finding out about me and Vincent.

"Because I am not worthy for the rank of Luna, because I was Rough before we met and, and, and..." I rolled my eyes.

He sighed. "So how did you end up with Vincent?"

I swallowed hard. "They wanted me to be some omega in pack, if it was up to them I would be the house maid. I would accept it. I left."

"And where does Vincent fit in?"

"He offered me a home and to get my son back. The held our boy and I wasn't allowed to see him."

He laughed. "Vincent doesn't simply just offer something at what prize, what did you give him Lea?"

"I..." I couldn't get the words out, my hart was pounding rapidly. Nathan raised an eyebrow at me. "I accepted to be his queen." Nathan didn't say anything. His expression fell, his jaw clenched. All he did was stand up, calmly and walked out the door.

"Nathan!" I called after him as I stood up.

"Let him be child." Isabella said. "He will calm down eventually."

I bolted towards the other door that led to the garden. I saw Vincent standing on a something that was almost a hill, looking out at the his fortune. I went to stand next to him.

"I told Nathan about our deal."

"Good, it's about time he finds out." Why was he so calm, does he not know the damage Nathan can cause him.

"Did you tell him about the other thing as well?"

"No."

"Keep it that way. I don't need some angry pup mad at me." Anger boiled inside me.

"Don't you think he is already angry?"

"Yeah but he will calm down soon, after you return to the pack."

"What makes you think I will return to the pack?"

"Were else do you plan to go. You ain't staying here. I have no more use for you, and I don't want Nathan marching here to get his queen back. Despite what you heard I really don't enjoy killing." Tears stung in my eyes. Why was he so mean.

"He will march here for his son!" I almost screamed.

"Oh that." He looked deep in thought. "You can keep the little mutt, I got what I wanted." I was livid and stomped away. The arrogance! Mutt? My wolf growled at that. I stomped all the way into Nathan's room. He looked shocked when he saw me.

"We are leaving for the pack. Now!"

He smirked at me, pleased with this declaration. I wasn't sure if I meant it. What guarantee do I have that this man, who felt like a stranger to me, was going to protect me against the rage and attacks from his pack. But staying at Vincents castle for one more second wasn't a option.

"Best get packing then." He responded. I turned and headed towards my room to begin packing. Something that Vincent said bothered me.

'I got what I wanted.'

Chapter 24 - An alpha's blood

A s soon as we came back to the pack house we were greeted with stares. As Nathan passed the wolves they all bowed their heads in respect but no one uttered a word. The house was silent. I held Aden tighter to me. Nathan headed straight to his office, Alec eyes widened when he saw him.

"What is this shit that my mate and your Luna be unranked?" This was the first words that Nathan had spoken since we got back.

"Alpha I was only doing what was best for our pack." Alec defended standing from the desk.

"And where the hell do you get that from?" Nathan spat.

"Alpha she is an outsider, she does not belong here."

"She is my mate! And your Luna, show her some respect. As if now she is given her position back as Luna."

"Yes Alpha." Alec submitted.

"And as for your punishment, you will work a week of kitchen duty."

What?!

"Alpha that is beneath me, I can't work as a commoner, what would the pack think! A beta in the kitchen. It's laughable."

"You will do as your told." He used his Alpha tone. Alec only nodded and left.

"Kitchen duty!?" I almost screamed. Isabelle who was clearly behind us took Aden and left with John.

"Whats the problem?" Nathan sat down at the desk.

"He basically threw me out of the pack and all he get is kitchen duty!"

"Lea, He was only doing what he thought was right. I probably would have done the same, I can't punish a beta on working on his instincts. Heck this was almost to harsh on him, but he must learn not to disrespect whats mine." I was beyond livid.

"Well technically I am NOT yours." I spat as I stormed out of the room slamming the door behind me.

That night Nathan came cautiously to bed. I already lied in bed when he entered. He stripped and got in next to me.

"Sorry." He whispered. I ignored him. "I cannot punish him, my pack would think my loyalty lies more with you than him, that I would ban my beta just because he had the pack in mind. Lea I can't."

I turned to face it. "Let's just leave it. I am still not happy with it, but I learned to let a lot of things go these last couple of months."

"Okay." He placed a hand on my waist, kissing my forehead. He didn't move after that, his face was incredibly close to mine.

"When you said today that you weren't mine. Memories flashed back from a night on a mountain top, where I asked you to be mine and you said yes." His face moved closer. My heart was pounding heavily. "I remembered how much I wanted you that night." He moved closer until our lips were almost touching. "How much I crave you!" He growled smashing his mouth on mine. I let the pleasure of him sink into me. I remembered most of our lives together, our talks, our kisses, our lovemaking. He moved down towards my neck and my collarbone, where the mark used to be, it had faded in time. He kissed it softly. And then he let his canines sink into that spot, both pleasure and pain shot threw me. He remarked me as his own .

******"Alpha!" A voice called knocking on the door.

"Yes!" Nathan growled his voice was husky, he was clearly in the mood for more sleep. He held my naked body tighter to him.

"There is a man here, a trader. He says he was valuable information. All he asks his food and a night to sleep."

"Send him away, I don't want anything." Nathan said shut his eyes again.

"He said its about Mia." Nathan sat up and got out bed, immediately started dressing. Nathan never told me how he escaped Mia. I must remember to ask him.

When we got downstairs, a scrawny little man dressed in rags sat at the kitchen table munching on food.

"Don't waist my time." Nathan said fierce to the man. He nodded repeatedly before answering.

"Apparently she marches toward you, she gathered a bunch of rouges and made an alliance with the Alpha's from the west and south wing. I saw them on my way here. They are a lot. She is sour because of your escape. You guys killed a lot her best fighters but she had time to revive. The witched left her , they said she is a lost cause, so the only magic that remains is hers. But she is powerful."

I looked at Nathan.

"How did you escape?"

"Isabella put some sort of mesmerizing spell on the weak minded soldiers and the strong minded ones I killed." He shrugged. "The hardest part was finding you, I met a member of the pack, a omega, along the way he said you left the pack. I didn't know where to start searching. I wanted to ask Vincents help." The mention of Vincent sent guilt inside of me.

"Oh Vincent the guy with the hybrid army?"The man who I forgot was still in our company said.

"He doesn't have a hybrid army, the experiments didn't work." I said bored.

"Oh, but he does. Apparently he got his hands on a very strong Alpha's blood. One that has not been heard of before. He injected the blood into the hearts of his soldiers so that they can be strong enough to take the pressure of a vampires blood. At least that's what I heard."

I got up and rushed towards my son's room. I saw he was a bit blue on his arm with a tiny injection mark. Son of a bitch!

Nathan came in.

"That asshole took Aden's blood for his army."

"I will kill him." Nathan snapped.

"Wait there's more." Now is as good time as any to tell him. "I slept with Vincent."

Chapter 25 - Heir for a Vampire?

Avoiding Alec was the hardest part of my morning. I had to eat, but him serving me wasn't pleasant because all I got was scowls and growls. I don't know if the rest of the pack are happy to see me here but all of them were respectful. All that Nathan had said to me since last was him not allowing me to sleep in another bed. He wasn't at breakfast, that earned suspicion from the rest of the pack. I made up the excuses but they didn't seem to buy it.

After breakfast I headed to the training ground. It was about time I start with my training again. Lou was already waiting for me, as soon as I came near he threw me a bamboo stick, it was heavier than I expected. I was contemplating its weight when Lou launched himself forward to me. I was so shocked I fell backwards and landed on my butt.

"Always be on your guard." He barked. I got up and took the bamboo in both hands standing on my guard. We sparred for what felt like forever. Every inch of me hurt by the time we were done and I headed upstairs to shower. After the shower I put on a bronze loose T-shirt and jean and headed to find Nathan we must talk this out.

As soon as I opened the door I was greeted by two eyes. Vincent and Nathan. Vincent's eyes was fixed on me which earned he growl from Nathan. Vincent turned his attention back to Nathan ignoring me.

"As I said." He continued. "There is no way in hell, you are going to use my hybrid army for your silly little war."

"And like I said it is my son's blood flowing through their veins!" Nathan stepped dangerously close.

Vincent looked at me again. He kind of looked like he zoned out, he does that when he thinks deeply

"Fine." He finally answered. "But I want something in return."

"What?" Nathan gritted threw his teeth.

"A vision from the seer."

"What!?" Nathan and I said in unison.

"You heard me."

"I can't do that. I don't know how to turn it off and on." I said.

"You better figure it out soon."

"Perhaps I can help." John interrupted walking into the room. "Sorry I wanted to talk to you Alpha and overheard."

"Continue" Was all Nathan said.

"Back when I was still an apprentice to the shaman, during the rein of your great grandfather, there were plenty of seer's around. I had become acquainted with one, back then they were called Oracle's. I saw how she preformed the ritual for a vision from the moon goddess. We can recreate it for you Luna."

"Hurry then. I will be waiting." Vincent said prompting himself on the couch taking out his phone.

"What do we need?" Nathan asked.

"Copper or gold or silver, basically anything that can generate energy and some wolfsbane."

"Wolfsbane? For what? Its poison to a wolf."

"She would have to take a little bit of it, not a lot, but a little."

"No I would not allow it."

"Nathan it's okay, I can handle it." I stepped closer to him. He sighed and nodded his head.

"Great I'll start making the wolfsbane into a drink and you go find the materials."

"For whats the rest?"

"As soon as the wolfsbane is in your system your energy levels would be low, subconsciously you start to channel the energy from the rocks."

"Oh."

"We would also need to clear out a room, there can't be any distractions."

"Fine we will have it handled." Nathan said.

****Later in room in the basement sat me and Vincent alone. A bunch of copper rocks were in front of me and a glass filled with wolfsbane and other ingredients. John explained everything to me.

"What do you want me to see?" I asked Vincent.

"Vampires can't have children right? But every king needs a heir. I want you to see if it would ever be able for me to have a heir." Maybe that's why he wanted my son? Other than taking his blood without permission.

"That's kind of wishy washy."

"Just try it okay."

"Fine." I looked down at the glass and took it in my hands and swallowed it with one sip. My vision started to blur. I could feel the energy seeping into my body. The next thing I knew there was a woman in front of me.

She had silver hair, white eyes and a very pale skin. She looked young and beautiful.

"Who are you?" I asked

"You know who I am child." Her voice was soft, almost like a melody. I did know who she was. The moon goddess.

"Do you have your question?"

"Yes my lady."

"Then close your eyes." I did as she asked. She touched my forehead and I was gone.

I woke in a field. Hybrids were training. It didn't look like Vincent castle, it was a lot bigger. That ass got what he wanted. In the field a very young woman stood out, a teen. She was fighting trying to prove she was the best between all the men.

"Esmeralda!" A voice screamed. Vincent's.

She rolled her eyes. "Dad." She responded.

"How many times do you I have to tell you, you cannot train with them!" He looked older when he appeared but not very much because vampires don't age really.

"And how many times do I have to tell you..."

"Let her be." A woman interrupted, taking position next to Vincent, she was a hybrid.

The vision ended. I woke up on Vincent's lap with him stroking my hair.

"I was worried." He said lifting me off. "You were gone for a long time."

I sat in front of him still weary because of the wolfsbane.

"I saw your answer."

"Okay."

"You will have a heir." I didn't really want to tell him it was a girl, seeing his reaction with her training I didn't know if he would be pleased. "The mother was a hybrid."

"That doesn't make sense! Hybrid or not I can't have children?"

"That is all she showed me sorry."

"It's okay." He stood up and helped me up. "Let's go get your army ready."

*****seriously guys, English is not my first language and if I tend to make mistakes please let me know.

Chapter 26 - Misguided

Nathan was waiting for us when we got outside the room, his whole body was tense. He clearly didn't like the idea of me and Vincent in the same room together. Vincent on the other hand was still confused as to what I had just told him, I personally don't even know how that is possible. I feel sorry for Vincent now knowing he wanted my son to be his own, but when that didn't work he moved to plan B.

"Your army will be ready tomorrow." Vincent looked at Nathan and started walking towards the exit. I was left alone with Nathan in complete silence. He still hasn't calmed down.

"You will follow into battle, at my side." He finally spoke up.

"What!?" As much as I want to rip Mia's head from her body for what she had done to us, I wasn't a warrior.

"I am hoping all you training with Lou actually meant something."

"Nathan do you not remember how all the seers got killed, because a foolish Alpha thought he can take them into war."

"I will protect you."

"Yeah right, he probably said that line too."

Suddenly Nathan was in front of me not even leaving space for a needle between us. "I will protect you with my life, if you would die, than so shall I."

I fell silent. Didn't know how to respond. At least he still cared about me, I hope. He placed a tiny kiss on my forehead.

"Come let's go train."

"Uh, I think Lou is busy with the front line warriors now, I saw them earlier heading that way."

"I didn't say you would be training with Lou." He winked and started walking towards the training fields.

In the middle of the fields there was a ring, commonly used for sparring and challenges. Nathan entered the ring and waited for me to approach. As soon as I was in the ring, I was face first on the ground, somehow being tripped by Nathan.

"Your enemy will not wait for you to enter the battlefield before attack, your enemy does not have morals, he is a coward, that makes him all the more dangerous. You must be on your guard at all times." I stood up growling flinging myself at Nathan, he stepped away and I fell again.

"Do not let emotions control your actions, that's when you make mistakes." I stood up again this time, I was standing in a fighting position ready for him to attack first. He stood there with his hands behind his back, calmly.

"Good now you are ready for a battle." He stepped closer to me, aiming a punch my way, I had just dived in the right time. It went on like that for a while, Nathan aiming punches, me trying to miss or block them. That's when I saw my opportunity. I launched a kick his way, but he grabbed my leg. Pulling me closer my one leg now on his waist with his hand moving towards my thigh. His other free hand he moved to my other thigh lifting me up on top of him. His hands positioned on my butts.

We just stood like that starring in to each others eyes, when his lips crashed into mine. I happily kissed him back not caring who was watching. I would even take him, there and now if it meant he would not be angry with my anymore. Our lips moved entwined, like they were made for each other, our sweaty bodies pressed hard together. This kiss was not passionate but rough. He bit my bottom lip asking me permission to enter my mouth, I parted my mouth, letting his tongue slip in, exploring me. I was disappointed when he pulled away, letting my feat back to the ground. Our breathing was heavy, his lips were swollen and red and I knew mine looked worse.

"What do you say we continue this back in our room?" He whispered with a husky voice in my ear. We both sort of smirked at each other before taking his hand and him leading me the way.

*******For the first time in a long time I felt happy again. Nathan was tracing my naked body with he fingers while I lied my head on his chest. My one hand playing with his soft hair, the other resting on his rock hard stomach. My eyes was closed breathing in his scent. I wished we could stay like this forever. There was a knock on the door. Nathan groaned and I tried my best to cover myself. Even though Nathan was sitting on most of the sheets and he was heavy.

"What?!" His voice ran through the room.

"A..alpha your son."

"What about him?" Nathan said sitting up straight.

"He seems to have a fever."

"Call the pack doctor and the shaman immediately, tell them to meet me in his room. NOW!" Nathan got up in the speed of light and got dressed. I did the same.

Before we even entered the baby's room we could hear the baby coughing. I took him in my arms and felt he was burning hot. The doctor approached with the shaman and John behind him.

"Lets have a look." The doctor told me, not really wanting to hand my child over, but I had to. The doctor examined him.

"Hmm beside the burning up and coughing, nothing else seems to be out of order. I would give you something for the fever, and then we will see in a couple of days." The doctor said.

"Shaman can you look if this is something magical. I am done with these games." Nathan said.

"Let me see." He stood over the child, eyes closed, slowly humming with his hands above the child.

"I sense no magic Alpha." He said. That was a relieve. Nathan order everybody out except me and him. We sat with our ill child.

"Excuse me?" John entered after a while. We both looked up at him. "I have to tell you something." Nathan nodded for him to continue.

"While the shaman did his thing, I decided to do my own check. I sensed magic, I don't know why he is hiding it from you, but he sure is laying."

Then it all made sense! How Mia easily had gotten herself in and out of our lands, how she knew exactly when to take Nathan, why he couldn't find a solution to the hex. The shaman is a traitor!

Chapter 27 - Surprise, surprise

This may be more violent chapter, just a warning.

As soon as we got to the shaman house he had already left. He knew that we were coming for him.

"Hey." Nathan said wrapping his arms around my waist. "We will find him I promise." He placed a kiss on my mark, a shiver went through my body. I closed my eyes in the pleasure.

"I just can't believe it! He helped us, he was my friend." Tears burned in my eyes. I just couldn't get over the betrayal. But I guess I should be used to it by now.

"Beautiful, I know it hurts but we will make him pay." I sighed and nodded, turning around and placed my head on his chest. He pulled me closer to him, kissing my head.

We stood like that for minutes, until I pulled away.

"Lets go get breakfast?" Nathan nodded and took my hand leading me towards the kitchen. The pack, or better yet the upper part of the pack worthy of eating breakfast with the Alpha and his Luna, was sitting there. There eyes was starring at us when we entered. Clearly the news of Mia and the shaman had spread.

"John." John looked up at Nathan curious. "You will be the new shaman until you can find and train someone else, that is if you accept." He nodded in approval.

"As for the rest of you. I am Alpha. I have never let you down and never will. We will find Mia and the other traitors and rip them to shreds! We will show them our power and why we are famous!" His motivation seemed to work. There was cheers, howls and battle cries sounding from the men and woman.

"And this time..." He looked at me smiling and held out a hand, I took it without thinking twice. "My queen and your luna will join us. By my side." My stomach turned at the thought of going into war. "We will raise, we will fight and we will kill. Victory is ours! Tonight we feast like kings, tomorrow we fight in war!" Tomorrow?. The crowd roared. It worked they were ready to fight and kill for there Alpha.

When me and Nathan were finally alone after a long day of training and a long night of drinking and dancing, I saw my opportunity.

"Tomorrow!?" I almost yelled.

"Yeah?" He shrugged.

"You could have told me! I am not ready I would get killed."

"I will protect you." He growled.

"You can't focus on me and a war!?"

"Calm down love, the packs needs their Luna and with her in their war, it inspires them. I will sacrifice my life for yours and our sons but this has to happen." The rest of the night I couldn't really remember, I just know sleep wasn't a big option.

"Five more minutes!" I said as I felt someone shaking me. Don't they know how important sleep is?

"It's time darling." Nathan's voice was ringing in my ears.

"Time for what?" I said turning, pulling the pillow over my head.

"War." He spoke coldly.

I sat up immediately, my heart racing. I forgot about the war. Nerves was creeping up towards me. Nathan noticed my distress and pulled me towards him kissing my forehead.

"Relax love, everything will be alright."

I got up and dressed. I doesn't really matter what I would be in wolf form anyways.

As soon as I got out the closet my vision became blurry.

Men are falling around me, Nathans wolf was beside me a deep red. I kept on running beside him, attacking everybody in our way. They dropped like sticks at our combined power. I have never seen so much blood in my life.

Mia stood on top of a hill we followed her as she ran when she saw us. She was afraid. When we got to the hill magic hit Nathan, he fell to the ground. Me and Mia circled each other waiting for one to attack. I launched forward first. Me and Mia was rambling on the ground trying each to get a bite out of each other.

The vision was gone. Nathan? Was he killed hurt? Was this a warning? I have to see him.

*****I couldn't see Nathan before the war. We marched and Nathan was at the back of the pack. We wanted me in front to let his people know that their leaders got them from the back and the front.

When we arrived at the destination we where greeted by Mia's warriors. She stood in the middle looking fierce dressed in all black leather. This was it. The time has come. When he came to a hold Nathan joined me in front taking my hand.

"It's not to late Mia." Nathan called out. "A war can still be avoided, just surrender and your death will be quick and painless."

"Never. I would kill the both of you even if its the last thing I do. Lea you first for taking my love. And you dear sweet Nathan for making a whore your mate!"

Footsteps were heard from the west. All our heads swung that way when Vincent and his hybrid army arrived. Just on time. Instead of Mia having a look of fear on her face she was smiling. At the back of her other gruesome creatures immersed, I recognized them from John's novels. Wendigo, me and my wolf thought in unison.

"Nathan my love." Mia's smile grew."Did you really think you are the only one who can make alliances?" Oh shit. Why couldn't the moon goddess have shown me this instead. I mentally face palmed.

Without a second thought Nathan marched forward with his men and Vincent following behind. I tried my best to stay at his side.

After what felt like hours it happened. Men were falling around me. Nathan's deep red wolf beside me, Mia on top of the hill fearing for her life, she started to run.

"Wait!" I called as Nathan followed but he didn't hear. I ran after him.

"Nathan wait!" I tried calling but it didn't help he kept on running and running until bam. The magic hit him. Me and Mia were now facing each other. She started to move and I followed facing her. We were starting to circle each other. This was it! I launched forward. The fight when on. She was channeling something because I felt my power leaving my body. I looked over at Nathan who was still laying there. Somehow that motivated me, I got more strength, overpowering Mia, until I was on top of her.

"I hope you enjoy hell." I said as I bit down at her, my canines sinking into her neck. I kept on going until her body stopped moving.

Once I looked up I saw her warriors retreating, the shaman was with them until Lou caught him and ripped out his heart.

I ran to Nathan. He started waking up. He looked shocked at me with my fur and mouth covered in blood. I changed back into my human form and so did he. In help him up and we looked at our pack with pride on the hill. They all bowed down towards us and started to howl. Me and Nathan howled with them. It was over. We had won then war.

So what happened after that was simple. Me and Nathan ruled the pack while raising our son. He became strong and fierce. Just like his dad. Nathan and I, well our flame was never extinguished. We had two daughters and another son as well. I don't want to sound cliché, but we lived happily ever after.

www.ingramcontent.com/pod-product-compliance
Lightning Source LLC
Chambersburg PA
CBHW070405200726
48294CB00003B/1094